Where Tillerman Rides

When rugged Sam Tillerman returned home to settle a family dispute with his estranged wife, he expected it to be done and dusted in days. Quick, tough and fast; that was Big Sam.

He had no way of knowing his return would coincide with that of desperado Struther Cady. Heading back to recover the $20,000 he'd stolen from the local bank, Cady was fresh from spending ten years in jail for robbery. Big Sam had no interest in any of this – until his daughter's beau was linked with the outlaw and the big twenty. Suddenly he was up to his neck in trouble.

From then on, Tillerman would have to outshoot his enemies, both of whom toted six-guns with Tillerman's name on the bullets!

Where Tillerman Rides

Clint Ryker

A Black Horse Western

ROBERT HALE · LONDON

ISBN 0 7090 7756 4

Robert Hale Limited
Clerkenwell House
Clerkenwell Green
London EC1R 0HT

Typeset by
Derek Doyle & Associates, Shaw Heath.
Printed and bound in Great Britain by
Antony Rowe Limited, Wiltshire

CHAPTER 1

BIG MAN'S BRAND

He was prepared to kill if he had to.

That resolution was clear in the desperado's mind as he put Black Bluff behind him and followed the stage-line trail. Somehow he'd managed to survive several years on the owlhoot without putting anybody in a grave. But this was time to face reality. Up until today he'd been a small-timer, living in a shadow world where the dangers were limited but pickings were lean.

It was time he moved up in the world.

Today would be the biggest job he'd ever attempted, and jobs didn't get much bigger or more dangerous in this part of the country than hitting the Sugarman stage-line.

It was a clear hot morning and he wore a wide-brimmed black Stetson tugged low to shade gaunt features and vicious dark eyes. The road began to climb; scattered fragments of torn cloud floated in the sky, and though he'd promised to keep his mind blank and calm until he reached the hilltop where Willy Loman's ranch fence touched the trail, he found this impossible.

His pocket-watch told him it was nearing nine and his hand was shaking.

Right about this time the morning stage from Sageville would be loading up for the run to Black Bluff and should top out the hill above Rustler's Canyon at around noon – where he would be waiting.

He'd been thorough and was proud of it. He'd visited Sageville the previous day and discovered all he needed to know, namely that there would be no foreseeable delays in today's run, there would be the standard driver and shotgun guard, several passengers who were of no importance; one who surely was.

Cleat Morgan had been winning big at the Sageville tables. He was Black Bluff's top gambler and played for high stakes. The Sageville rumour mill calculated his winnings there at well over $5,000 – and this lean and hungry stick-up man would gun his own granny for less.

The horse tossed its head and jerked sideways as a small red snake slid across the yellowish-red earth, sinister and sleek in the dust.

The rider was calm again as he fingered gun butt.

Of course, Morgan had a reputation for being as slick with a Colt as he was with a deck of cards, he reflected. But that didn't faze him. He was a long way better than slick, and would have the advantage of surprise.

They would never know what hit them.

*

The Saturday stage was overdue but one man who saw the bright side of this was Black Bluff's resident bum, No Dollars Flynn. Days like this, men bought drinks for the old-timers down on their luck, and No Dollars' taste for hard liquor guaranteed that tossing of drinking silver every day of his life. No job all year. Sponged drinking money from his niece who tended bar at the Big Dipper. No friends in town, but sometimes he got lucky with strangers.

Visits to two of the town's three saloons found him just as broke and even drier than on starting out, which only left the Indian Queen directly opposite the depot-landing, where people were waiting for the noon stage to come rolling in.

No luck at the Queen either, and No Dollars was chewing ruefully on his moustache and wondering how folks could be so concerned about a lousy stage being a lousy hour late when he had real problems – when the sheriff showed.

The louvered doors of the saloon opened on well-oiled hinges and Tad Henry entered with his polished star pinned to his jacket lapel, touching the waxed tips of his moustaches. Black Bluff's peace officer was something of a dandy but tough enough and more than confident in his ability to handle both hardcases and pretty women alike. This assurance showed in the way he dressed in broadcloth coat and natty vest, and drinkers gave way to him now as he made for the bar, for that was just the way things were in this hot high-plains town in the summer of '85.

7

The lawman halted alongside glum No Dollars to run a shrewd eye over the visitors to his town. He spoke from the corner of his mouth:

'I'll buy you a shot for every sneak thief you spot for me.'

Flynn vanished in a twinkling, and the curly-headed bartender came up behind the sheriff and placed two fingers on the mahogany.

'Cain't recall when it was this late before, Sheriff.'

'Huh?' Henry was vague. He'd just caught a fleet-ing glimpse of somebody who looked familiar, vanishing through the doors of the Riata across the street. Someone female. 'What was that?'

'The stage. Sixty-five minutes overdue now, Sheriff.'

Henry frowned at the man then smiled at the whiskey. He downed it with a flick of the wrist, set down the empty glass, shot his cuffs.

'You worry too much, my friend,' he counselled. 'In my experience, stagecoaches are like in-laws. Always turn up eventually.'

Even if the barman might not agree with this example of tin-star wisdom, he wouldn't say so. Tad Henry was genial but tough, friendly but tetchy-vain. But because he did such a fine job of maintaining law and order here he could be droll or supercilious most any time he wanted.

The lawman glanced along the street in the direc-tion the stage would appear, yet his mind was else-where. At the Riata, to be exact. Where had he seen that shimmering head of vivid red hair before?

As he approached the Riata he encountered citizens gathered in knots, doubtless discussing the stage. Inside, it was hot. Drinkers lined the bar but the gambling layouts were largely unattended. The men at the bar drank whiskey-shots from small glasses, passing the bottle restlessly. This was the early afternoon lull between late-morning need and the energy and optimism of early evening.

'Don't tell me,' Henry said to the busty blonde bargirl as she made to speak. 'The stage is late – and where's that redhead?'

The girl poured him a beer but couldn't help him concerning the woman. Couldn't or wouldn't, perhaps. Black Bluff was not a large town and eligible bachelors were rare as hen's teeth, with the impressive and well-respected Henry rating high in that category. The lawman could do worse than pay her a little attention, the girl was thinking, but he was unaware of her annoyance as he surveyed the familiar surroundings. A fish hawk was suspended in full flight above the back mirror, wings stiffly out from supporting wires. Above the stuffed bird was an ancient and faded campaign poster: LINCOLN AND THE UNION.

Suddenly she appeared, sweeping in from an alcove trailed by a couple of admiring gamblers; tall, vital and striking in a slightly larger-than-life way, the redhead the sheriff had glimpsed from afar several times over the past month on his streets, was even more striking at close range. Immediately he began searching for a name as she headed for the batwings. Mary . . . Monica . . . Marie. That was it. Marie Elena Sanchez, a flamboyant name for a lovely creature who lit up the drab Riata like a Roman candle.

'Miss Sanchez,' he called, deserting the bar. 'Might I be of assistance?'

'Don't bother me, sonny,' she replied, then slowed when she saw the badge on his lapel. She forced a smile, and naturally it was dazzling. 'Pardon me, Sheriff. You'd be Tad Henry, right?'

He felt ridiculously pleased that she knew his name. He took her gloved hand and bowed to kiss it. This was supposed to send any woman weak at the knees, but when he raised his eyes to hers he found her twinkling with tolerant amusement. 'Why, Sheriff, what a slinky little saloon-lizard you turned out to be.'

His cheeks burned as he straightened stiffly. Someone sniggered. He was ready to be offended when his eyes strayed to what was possibly the most seriously carnal set of breasts he'd seen in far too long, daringly revealed by a low-cut bodice for all the world to see.

'Miss Sanchez, I—'

'You'll have to save it, Sheriff cutie. The stage is coming in – at long damn last.'

'How do you know?'

Marie Elena cupped a hand to her ear and said: 'Listen.'

The lawman did as he was told, and sure enough, above the murmur of saloon and street he picked up the distinct sound of hoofs and wheels clattering hollowly across the river bridge in back of McCall Street.

'Allow me,' he insisted, and held the doors open

10

for them to step through together just as Tillerman brought the Concord rocking around the hotel corner a block away.

The crowd at the saloon here didn't realize it was Sam Tillerman plying the reins and driving far too fast as the rig and six straightened up for the run to the depot. But further along, they recognized the driver right off. Yet despite the big man's high profile on his occasional visits to their town, they were far more interested in regular driver Barney Flood as he swayed ashen-faced upon the spring seat at Tillerman's side clutching a bloodied shoulder and looking grey as old sawdust.

'Get out of my goddam way and get the doc, damn your eyes!'

At six-three in height and a yard wide across the shoulders, Big Sam Tillerman had lungs to match the rest of him. His shout touched off a wave of alarm and excitement ahead of the lathered team, and Black Bluff's medico left his sourmash half-drunk as he snatched up his little black bag and came trotting from the Blind Pig, coughing in the hoof-lifted dust.

Tillerman continued to let the teamers have their heads until within fifty feet of his destination. Only then did he bellow: 'Whoa!' and throw his full weight back on the reins to manhandle the team to a sliding, dust-billowing halt flush with the landing.

'Damned show-off fool!' muttered the sheriff, causing his stunning companion to whirl on him with fire in her eye.

'What did you say, Sheriff Lecher?' she challenged testily.

11

'Er, I . . . well—'

'Who cares anyway?' The redhead dismissed him. Then, throwing her arms wide, she shouted at the coach: 'Tillerman! Just what do you think you're doing now?'

'Red!' Tillerman bawled back, standing to tower high above the whole dusty, animated scene. He shot her a salute before directing his attention to the crowd on the landing.

'Up by Rustler's Canyon,' he stated. 'Where the limestone ends and the trace begins again. Tucked away in those cottonwoods by Willy Loman's fence, he was. The road agent. Damnedest thing. We were weaving into the corner and suddenly this gunner cuts loose, wings the driver sitting right next to me, then plugs Cleat Morgan taking a doze inside. . . .'

At this point his words were lost in the uproar as it was realized a second man was wounded. And not just anybody either. Cleat Morgan was Black Bluff's gambling boss to whom at least half the men present owed money.

Tillerman sprang to ground and shrugged off the back-slappers, forcing his way clear of people rushing to the aid of the wounded. He heaved a gusty sigh as he thrust his hat back from his brow to release a pool of sweat. Late forties, bronzed and brawny with the seamed face of a headlong liver of life, Tillerman towered above most around him. He was using his height now to try and spot his redhead again when somebody tugged at his sleeve.

'Mr Tillerman, who was the dirty, dry-gulchin' sonuva who done the shootin'?'

'Easy, son, easy,' Tillerman barked. 'Don't speak ill of the dead.'

'You killed him?' demanded the sheriff.

'Killed him, drilled him, whatever,' came the brusque reply. 'I cut loose and he fell in a heap, that's all that signifies. Hey, Red!'

Whatever Sheriff Tad Henry wanted to say to her at that moment was lost as Marie Elena burst through the mob to be swept up in Tillerman's arms and swung in a wide, petticoat-flurrying arc which almost succeeded in knocking the lawman off his feet.

'What a man!' someone enthused loudly, but nobody seemed to hear the sheriff of Black Bluff say with rare feeling:

'What a limelighter!'

They say a man is never a hero to his valet. Nor, it would seem in this case, to the local sheriff.

If there was one thing Sam Tillerman could do better than most it was have a good time. Dumped in the middle of the desert a hundred miles from anyplace it was a fair bet that he could scare up company, liquor and at least one lively female by next day's noon at the latest. Leastwise that was what they said about him here and there. But things were not that primitive in Black Bluff, where three bustling saloons, a dance-hall, gambling-parlour and two small, discreet whorehouses ensured that this was a place where anybody was welcome to have fun providing he confined his hell-raising to the limits of the law.

That night he started things off by treating Red to champagne at the Plains Hotel. He followed this up with a shave, trim, hot tub and rub-down at the hotel by which time he'd put away half a bottle of bourbon – and one sick and sorry dry-gulcher had been hauled into town on the back of a flat-bed wagon. Somehow the badman had survived Tillerman's fusillade but was feeling so bad he almost wished he hadn't.

It was something to see as Tillerman, togged out in fresh gear with a freshly lighted cigar between his teeth and a radiant Marie Elena on his arm, allowed himself to be drawn from the Indian Queen by an acclaiming mob to supervise the outlaw's offloading at the law office.

Everyone cheered, the shot-up road agent hung his sorry head and bled a little, Tillerman acknowledged the plaudits with some modesty, while the sheriff sounded about as tetchy as a man could get as he took the miscreant into custody and bawled for the medic.

From this ego-boosting interlude to the dance-hall was just a short step, and men in boiled white shirts and women in frills and flounces looked on and marvelled that a man of Tillerman's often intimidating personality and turbulent background, fresh from a victorious Colt argument with a two-gun dry-gulcher, could give himself over to music and dancing so completely you'd think he didn't have a serious bone in his body.

There was ample fuel for gossip amongst citizens who'd not seen the big man from Turlock County in over a year, and those in the know were quick to bring less well-informed newcomers up to date on just who and what they were watching doing the stately

Gordon and the rafter-rattling Irish jig to the stirring back-home beat of the Black Bluff Guitar Band.

The picture they painted was of a pioneer cattle baron, former family man divorced from a woman even more striking than Red Sanchez – so they claimed – now operating as some kind of high-rolling trouble-shooter for various combines as well as dealing widely in cattle and horses who managed to attract trouble, acclaim, publicity and notoriety in roughly equal amounts as he criss-crossed the High Plains with the restless energy and headlong drive of a man half his age.

Whether or not Tillerman enjoyed his renown nobody seemed to know for sure, although it was often pointed out that if he was any kind of shrinking violet he did a damn fine job of concealing it.

It seemed expected and inevitable that the eye-catching couple should visit both the Indian Queen and the Riata before taking a candlelight midnight supper at the Plains Hotel, where the kitchen staff had been kept on to supply Tillerman's favourite dish – buffalo-hump steak with everything.

The street was quieter now. The Queen had shut down but there was still a bunch of drinkers setting them up and knocking them back over at the Riata as they continued to discuss the attack on the stage.

Sheriff Henry had been busy, and had discovered that the road agent's intention had been to hold up the noon stage and rob Morgan, believed to be returning from the South with serious money on his person.

15

With three wounded men to care for, the doctor was still making his rounds as three well-primed cowboys rode from the Cleveland Corral, heading home to the Walking Nine. Their way led past a row of darkened stores and the brightly lighted telegraph office where they never closed down.

Most nights, unless otherise engaged romancing some fresh young country girl, buxom widow woman or somebody whose husband was out of town on a business trip, the sheriff would be abed by this, being an early riser and long-day worker. Not tonight.

With lights turned low and his patched-up prisoner bombed out of his skull on laudanum and a few generous whiffs of ether, Tad Henry sat with chair tilted back, spurred boots on the desk and glass in hand, staring directly across the street at the glowing windows of the hotel, occasionally catching a snatch of laughter from within, female laughter more often than not.

The lawman dropped his boots and leaned forward with a worried frown as the dining-room lights were first dimmed, then turned out.

And well he might worry.

At that moment, a smiling desk clerk was watching the most striking couple the Plains had paid host to in some time, making their way slowly up the carpeted stairs, arms about one another's waists, red head snuggling brawny shoulder. The clerk sighed. He was a skinny spotty man of twenty-one but a romantic at heart. How come an 'old guy' nearing fifty so seemingly effortlessly swept up such a stunner as the fiery Chavez beauty, when he couldn't get one

16

of Madam Effie's tough chippies to drape herself all over him in that sexy way even if he paid for it?

What did Big Sam Tillerman have that he didn't?

He was still enumerating the long list of possible answers to his own query a short time later when he looked up in surprise at the sound of steps to see someone entering the lobby.

The nightcomer raised a clatter but the normally alert Tillerman didn't hear a thing. Didn't want to hear anything but their own heavy breathing as button-hooks clicked open and footwear was discarded in a hurry in the bridal suite fifteen feet above.

'Sweet glory, Tillerman, it's been too long, damn you, way too long.'

He let her talk as he swept her up in his arms and carried her to the huge double bed where slanting moonlight fell across the rose-colored carpet in a gauzy blue haze.

As knuckles sounded on the door.

Tillerman stiffened. He didn't believe it! She did.

'Ignore it, Sam.' Marie Elena's voice was husky as she attempted to drag him down. 'Whether you believe it or not, I've been saving myself up for a real honest-to-God man ever since you wired me to meet you here a month ago. . . . I honestly have. . . . Even if it's the end of the world – who cares?'

How could he resist? And yet somehow he did. For Tillerman had left iron-clad instructions that they were not to be disturbed before ten in the morning under pain of death. He couldn't believe that weedy clerk would dare disregard such instructions unless – unless what?

The knock was repeated.

'Sorry, Mr Tillerman – urgent wire for you, sir!'

His gunrig was looped around a bedside chair. Fighting off love-famished Red with one hand, Tillerman groped for the Colt .45 with the other. He was cursing as he made his big-shouldered way through the half-darkness, his mood not improved when he stubbed a toe.

'What?' he shouted as his fingers closed over the smooth hardwood door handle. He jerked it open so violently the clerk jumped back two paces, holding an envelope up before him protectively when the passageway light fell on Tillerman's angry face.

'A w-wire for you, Mr Tillerman, sir.'

'You disturbed me for a telegram?'

'From a Mrs Caroline Tillerman, Tadpole Ranch, Turlock County, Mr Tillerman, sir!'

It was suddenly hushed as Tillerman lowered his six-gun. The silence was broken by a peeved voice from the gloomy room.

'What is it, Sam?'

'It's a wire from Mrs Tillerman, ma'am,' the jittery clerk informed unwisely. A curse sounded from in back of him yet Tillerman still seemed too surprised to react to anything. Then he shook his shoulders and snatched the envelope from the trembling clerk. He was tearing it open with big blunt fingers as the first piece of flying bedside crockery struck the jamb behind him and shattered into a hundred pieces.

Sheriff Tad Henry must have dozed off. He jerked his

head up with a start, blinking first at his turned-down nightlight, then at his comatose prisoner in the cell. He eventually turned his fuzzy gaze to the darkened front window from which he had been spying on the hotel.

He took one startled look, then was lunging for the door like like a sprinter coming out of the blocks. Just about any red-blooded man alive would surely do the same to take a closer look at Marie Elena Sanchez, red mane flowing and wearing nothing more than a light chemise as she shouted angrily from the hotel balcony.

Yet it was more what the woman was yelling, along with the puzzling sight of a fully attired Tillerman walking a rented horse around the corner from the livery that prompted the no-longer groggy lawman to cross his porch so openly. And now he could hear what the woman was saying, his puzzlement slowly gave way to a smirk which quickly became a smile.

'You are a liar and a sham, Sam Tillerman. You swore on a stack of Bibles it was all over with your snooty wife, but deep down I knew you were carrying a torch for her – you lying, low-down—'

'Damnit, Red,' Tillerman's big voice barked back as he paused mid-street. 'I've got to go, and anybody but a crackbrained redhead would know it if only she would only listen.'

'Cheating, lying pimp!'

'Are you going to listen or not?'

'That horse has more character than you do! And breeding.'

Tillerman filled leather, spun his mount in a tight

circle then took off along the main street at the gallop, leaving the woman still cursing, the desk clerk gaping from the hotel doorway, and the sheriff scarce able to believe his luck. Stately and reassuring, Sheriff Henry crossed the street and swiftly climbed to the balcony, both hands outstretched, expression radiating concern.

'Miss Marie Elena, allow me to extend my cond—'

'What are you?' she blazed, making a half-hearted attempt to close the gaping chemise. 'Some kind of pervert? Can't you see the way I'm dressed?'

A moment later she had disappeared. For a crazy moment, the sheriff was tempted to follow, then thought better of it. She was visibly upset – to put it mildly. But he was a patient man, tomorrow was another day, and, most significant of all, Tillerman was gone. And yet, pleased as he was, Tad Henry was intensely curious. For what in the world could possibly be important enough to drag any man away in the middle of a moonlit night from that voluptuous, sweet-scented vision he'd just seen?

It was both puzzling and aggravating, he decided. But then, that could be an apt description of Big Sam Tillerman's whole life. He told himself he really didn't give one sweet damn why the big man had gone, just so long as he never showed his face in his town again. This impressive man of the law would never admit that, any time he was around, Marie Elena's now-ex made him feel small.

CHAPTER 2

TEN YEARS ON

Tillerman stood with fists on hips and ankle-deep in the lush pile carpet he had once had shipped out all the way from New Orleans at a cost he didn't even want to think about now.

In truth all he could consider in that electrically charged moment of reunion here in the heartland of the empire of cattle, grass and men which he had moulded with his own hands, was the defiance of the woman standing facing him, and the astonishing words that had just come from her lips.

'Let me get this straight, Mrs Tillerman.' His tone was as ominous as that of a hanging judge clarifying a point of law prior to passing sentence. 'After not communicating with me in three months, and your being fully aware of my disinclination to share your assertive company in any circumstances, you took it upon yourself to lure me back here by way of a totally misleading message just to tell me that our daughter is dating? Correct me if I'm wrong, would you be so kind, madam?'

She'd always hated it when he adopted this deliberately overbearing manner and reached deep into his grab-bag of big words, trying to impress. But today Caroline Tillerman, mistress of Tadpole and former wife of its former master, had far too many other grave concerns to contend with to allow her anger full rein, something she was quite prone to do on many occasions.

'Dating?' she snapped, chewing on the word. 'Did I use the word "dating"? I am not talking dating, *Mr* Tillerman. I contacted you for the very real and serious reason that your daughter has become involved with a totally unsuitable man almost twice her age who just very well might be shady, possibly already wed, who could even be an outright criminal of some kind for all I know. Now, if you would be good enough to clean your ears out and pay attention—'

'Criminal, you say?' Tillerman's truculent pose was suddenly beginning to falter. When they had divorced, following several years of touchy skirmishing, abrasive character clashes and many a raging, blazing brawl interspersed with periods of truly remarkable passion, the most vitriolic point of contention between the Tillermans had not been the Tadpole itself. He'd handed the cattle kingdom over to her with scornful nonchalance, lock, stock and barrel and with no regrets. But their one child, the now eighteen-year old Trina, apple of the eyes of both parents, was a far different matter.

Tillerman had foolishly thought he might secure

custody of the girl in return for handing his wife the finest cattle outfit in Turlock County. Some hope. By the time Caroline and her fat attorney had finished with him in the courts, he was lucky still to have limited visitation rights. The couple had barely spoken or communicated since, she peeving him by running the spread as well as he had ever done, he getting back at her by continuing his hard-driving and highly successful way of life, his every word and action suggesting that he considered shucking a spread worth $100,000 to be free of her was worth every cent.

His daughter was Big Sam's Achilles heel. His ex-wife knew this and it was just possible that she used Trina as a weapon to hurt him or drag him down from his high horse as she had often done in the past.

Yet studying the classically beautiful face he knew so well, he had doubts. Surely Caroline would not stoop to that. There was a limit to how far they would allow mutual enmity to take them, and he believed that that line was drawn by their daughter.

Some of the iron tensions ran out of his big frame as Tillerman moved across the huge front room to the cold hearth, above which hung a life-sized oil-painting of himself in range gear astride his favourite horse from the good times.

'What is this man's name?' he said in a quieter tone, tight little white lines of concern showing at the corners of his mouth.

'Emile Santone.'

Tillerman swung sharply.

'I've heard that name someplace.'

'What did you hear?'

His bronzed brow furrowed in concentration.

'Can't rightly recall the details. But it seems to me whatever it was, it wasn't anything too flash.' He nodded. 'Better enlighten me.'

It turned out that in her characteristically thorough way, Caroline had managed to unearth a deal of information on Mr Emile Santone of Denver, Colorado. Through one of her ex-husband's few real friends, Sheriff Nate Poole of San Rafael, she had been able to learn that the man in question had a wide reputation in gambling circles, had been in jail in Nevada several years earlier, was a suspected consort of undesirables, possibly outlaws, and was considered a womanizer to boot. Add these facts to the reality that Santone had now been lodged lavishly at San Rafael's premier hotel for several weeks during which his prime occupations seemed to be playing cards and romancing the Tillermans' only daughter, and it was Caroline's considered opinion that she had every right to hit the panic button. Didn't he agree?

It mostly took more than this to induce Tillerman to agree to anything. But not this time. His expression was sober as he lowered himself to the big hand-carved grandfather chair that had once been his, reached for his cigars.

'You were quite right to inform me, Mrs Tillerman,' he said sombrely. He bit off the end of a cheroot, spat it into the hearth and slapped the patch-pockets of his denim shirt, searching for vestas.

His dark brows cut deep in a familiar black scowl. 'Staying at the Keylock Hotel, you say?'

'Yes. What are you intending to do, Samuel?'

His eyes were flinty now.

'I'll start off by having a few words with Mr Santone. You know, find out what his intentions towards Trina are.'

'And then?'

'That will depend a lot on Mr Santone's answers and what I make of them.'

'You haven't changed, have you, Samuel.'

'How's that?' he replied defensively. He knew that tone. Seemed that as they had grown older and richer together his wife had become more aware of his shortcomings and more ready to identify them for his benefit. He would never concede that he might have grown more headstrong, arrogant and difficult as he travelled the high road to success. As far as he was concerned he was the same man he'd been thirty years ago, punching cattle for the E.R. Barnes Stock Company down on the Texas panhandle.

'You're going to warn him off, and if that doesn't work you will break his jaw or leg or something. Correct?'

There was an edge of bitterness to the woman's tone. In the early years she had regarded her husband's two-fisted toughness as a necessary quality if they were both to achieve the goals they sought in a hard country where the prize went to the strong. But in later years this very characteristic had helped lead to friction and eventually the final rift.

Smoke rose in a sifting grey veil before Tillerman's powerful face. There was a quietness within the room that was exaggerated by the sharp bark of a dog out by the barn. He was thinking what a remarkable-looking woman she was still, yet he could see how the years, events, heartbreaks and responsibilities were turning the dew on this Irish rose to a diamond hardness.

'I'll do what has to be done,' he stated flatly. 'Like always.'

'Of course you will. But don't you think you should speak with your daughter first.'

'You said she isn't at home.'

'She will be back by evening.'

Tillerman rose with characteristic vigour and grabbed his hat from the staghorn rack.

'If I speak to Missy and tell her I'm concerned about her and this geezer, she will just get all fired up and tell me to mind my own business. But if I straighten things out beforehand, then I've trumped her, right? Right?'

Caroline's shoulders slumped. She was a full-figured, dark-haired woman of forty who had been rearing a daughter and bossing a 5,000-head spread alone for the past several years. Right at this moment she was stressed and edgy, yet was determined to control her at times uncertain Emerald Isle temperament. 'I sent for you so I'll support whatever steps you take,' she said with an air of finality, going to the double doors.

'Even if they might be wrong?' he challenged.

'Even if.' Caroline paused in the doorway before

26

leaving the room. 'Oh, and there's another thing you should know, Samuel. Struther Cady is back in San Rafael. Can you believe it's been ten years?'

Struther Cady!

The name from the past brought a real sting to the present for Tillerman as he let his rented horse carry him placidly along the oak-tree-lined trail for the town. For the moment it even outweighed his concern for his daughter and what would seem to be her real bad taste in men.

A decade earlier, in the winter of '75, a matched pair of Nevada badmen named Struther Cady and Lucas McCoy crossed the Line and pushed their stolen horses across a hundred miles of some of the most picturesque, snow-covered scenery in the Territory to light eventually upon the Turlock County town of San Rafael, home of the prosperous Westland Bank.

At that time moneys from the last spring's beef sales were flowing in and the Westland's vaults were bulging at their welded seams.

The robbery was cleverly planned and expertly executed, up to a point. Cady and McCoy were packing in excess of $20,000 cash when they quit the bank leaving behind them a bound and gagged manager and staff along with half a dozen immobilized customers.

It was the kind of clockwork operation to be expected of two seasoned professionals. They'd plundered banks, express offices and moneylenders' offices all over in the past and knew all the finer points. They didn't rush off from the bank following the hold-up, but rather strolled casually away, in order not to attract undue attention, down Springfield Lane to reach the sheltered lot where they had left their horses, only to find them gone.

Turned out Sheriff Nate Poole had come upon the mounts and, peeved because riders were continuing to ignore his city ordinance concerning random use of private unoccupied properties, had taken the animals off to the jailhouse stables where a fee fine would be levied before the owners got them back.

The badmen from Nevada weren't about to visit any jailhouse right then. Instead they went searching for the nearest available horses and found them in back of the saloon. They were taking off on two Circle J Ranch blood barbs when the alarm was raised after a customer strolled into the bank.

Those fine animals were about to cost two Nevadan badmen dear.

The alarm was raised.

Tadpole boss Tillerman and old pal Sheriff Nate Poole were in the forefront of the blazing gun-battle that erupted on Deacon Street as the robbers blasted their desperate way to freedom – of a kind. The lawman and the rancher subsequently headed up the the posse which gave furious chase and harried the bandits as far as Black Rock, where Struther Cady stopped a bullet in the hip and was brought crashing to ground. This left that sharp-shooting hardcase to stand off the manhunters alone at the rock while Lucas McCoy, also wounded but well mounted, hammered off in the direction of Dreamer's Mountain. Only one posseman dared brave Cady's lashing cover fire in order to cut around the toe of Black Rock and chase after McCoy, and that was Sam Tillerman astride the big bay gelding he used to ride back then.

Even then Tillerman had a reputation for impulsiveness and a two-fisted approach to everything he touched or got involved in. With his own funds invested in the plundered bank, with the sheriff as his best friend, and having seen two bleeding towners lying in the streets in the wake of the shoot-out, Tillerman was as fired up as he'd ever been that dangerous winter's afternoon. He had no intention of returning without the two-gunner providing his luck and the big strong gelding held up.

It was several hours and many dangerous miles later before exhaustion and a failing horse so slowed the deadly McCoy that his pursuer was able to draw within gun range of his quarry along the twisting line of Crawdad Creek linking Frog Hollow behind him and Marble Canyon several miles ahead in the rugged foothills of Dreamer's Mountain.

What followed was a brutal, ever-climbing running duel that took fugitive and pursuer out of the canyon in hock-deep snow to cross Buffalo Hump, down to Skeleton Wash, across the canyon again then up along precipitous Blue Hills Trail to Red Man's Draw . . . and onwards to a fateful unidentified spot higher up the mountainside. There, beneath a canopy of drifting gunsmoke, two desperate men fought it out in a brutal gundown that left Lucas McCoy stretched dead and defiantly half-smiling, with a wounded and blood-spattered Tillerman standing over him.

The badman had proved as gun-skilled and gutsy as reputation painted him but Tillerman's sheer relentlessness finally wore him down until he jumped up to shoot when he should have stayed put and tucked his head in.

Back in town the sheriff was holding a wounded Struther Cady under lock and key. The lawman also had in his possession the now empty bank-bag which an afoot Cady had been seen carrying, bulging, when he was taken at Black Rock Canyon at the end of his one-man, two-hour stand against the posse at Two Mile Rock.

That sack had been a ruse to convince the possemen at Black Rock that the encircled bandit was holding the money, when in fact McCoy had slipped away with it.

And stashed it somewhere between Crawdad Creek and Red Man's Draw.

Not one dollar of the Westland robbery was located then or later, despite a frenzy of searching, combing and digging, plus the subsequent strenuous efforts of legions of treasure-seekers that continued for years afterwards.

McCoy was lying stiff and stark on a slab at the undertaker's and a defiant Cady was swearing on Bibles that McCoy had taken the plunder with him when he left him alone and unhorsed to face the wrath of the posse, even though everyone, Tillerman in particular, knew this to be a bare-faced lie.

Due to the fact that McCoy was regarded as the brains behind the hold-up and had been responsible for the bloodshed during the run-out, Cady got off with the relatively light sentence of ten years' hard labour.

Tillerman had no inkling where the money had been hidden.

Over time, people from bank presidents and Territory Rangers down to every con he'd done time with tried to persuade the outlaw to reveal where his partner might have stashed the fortune.

'What can I tell you?' was his stock reply. 'Go ask McCoy.'

'But McCoy is dead.'

'May he rest in peace.'

Lighting up a fresh stogie as he splashed across Chaparral River at Hud's Crossing, Tillerman found it hard to believe that all that drama had taken place a full decade ago – when his little girl was just eight years of age and he and his wife were still in love.

His hard jaw set with a click. So a shadow from the past had returned just as he got back to the county. So what! He was here for one reason only and that had nothing to do with Struther Cady. He would stay focused on the job in hand and would not be letting up until Mr Emile Santone was out of his daughter's life and his ex-wife was forced to concede that his individual style of dealing with trouble always panned out to be the best.

He grinned at the thought of Caroline actually conceding this point, then frowned when for some reason Marie Elena Sanchez flashed into his thoughts. He realized quite involuntarily that, although he and just about everyone else regarded

Red as a knockout, when it came down to simple good looks, Mrs Tillerman was still streets ahead. For some reason this made him sore.

'To hell with it!' he barked, kicking the horse into a run. For the remainder of the journey he made certain he didn't allow his thoughts to touch on anything else but his daughter. And of course, Mr Emile Santone. That shady-sounding character was going to wonder what had hit him when 'daddy' buttonholed him.

Cady sure had a nerve!

Leastways that was the general opinion of the loafer bunch lounging around in the shade of the Ten Bar saloon's front porch that afternoon.

They'd heard the outlaw had shown up a couple of days earlier but there had been no more sightings of the former San Rafael bank-robber so now opinion was that he must have drifted on – which would seem a damn sensible thing to do, all things considered.

Then suddenly there the jailbird was, large as life and all too familiar to some, standing before the stage depot rolling a smoke just like any other citizen, drifter or Johnny-come-lately with nothing more important on his mind than where he might find a cold beer.

Ten years was a long time and most of the onlookers there today only knew Cady by reputation. But one man had actually been manhandled and hog-tied at Westland Bank that fateful afternoon, and he spat angrily in the hot dust and craned his neck left and right in search of the familiar and reassuring figure of the sheriff before bringing his disgusted gaze back into focus on the figure across the street.

'I jest don't believe it,' he said emotionally. 'Is he loco or somethin'? There are men here who might just plug that bastard on sight and I ain't sure if any judge would convict 'em.'

'Must be a nervy breed, seems to me,' opined a newcomer. 'That's if what all you boys have told me about that hold-up day is true.'

This remark touched off a sudden wrangle of voices with each man trying to outdo his neighbor with his recollections of the most notorious event in San Rafael history. Across the street the focus of their attention took a deep drag on his cigarette and made a conscious effort to appear harmless and inoffensive. This was not an easy thing to do for Struther Cady. For the marks of his calling were stamped deeply upon the lean and hungry Nevadan, in his deep facial lines and the feral glitter of ice-blue eyes set wide apart and watchful. He'd been a slender man of twenty-one the day he shoved a loaded gun into a teller's waistcoat button and demanded the keys to the vault. Now, with thirty years well behind him he was bronzed, hardened and grizzled after a decade spent smashing rocks and getting clubbed across the skull any time he so much as looked sideways by the bosses who knew exactly how to handle his breed.

Ten years spent halfway to hell. You'd expect, after that, all any man would want would be a little peace and quiet, an accommodating woman or two, the opportunity to lie in bed until sun-up – without some outsized yard-bull laying a cane against the soles of his naked feet and roaring in his ear fit to bust an eardrum.

'Rise and shine, you motherless scumsucker!'

Not Struther Cady, apparently.

According to Sheriff Poole's calculations based on the time of Prisoner 107's release, he must have quit the penitentiary and headed directly across country for San Rafael to get there as quickly as he had. Like he couldn't wait to hit a town where virtually everyone knew him and hated his guts!

Pretty bizarre. But then who would expect sensible behaviour from any low-life bank-busting outlaw anyway?

'Mornin', folks,' Cady said to the dignified man and woman coming arm-in-arm along the walk. He tipped his hat to the woman, nodded respectfully to her silver-haired husband. He might have saved himself the effort. The couple swept on by, noses in the air, the dignified gentleman muttering something under his fine silver moustache, the only word Cady heard clearly being 'vermin'.

He was lucky it was not much worse. The citizen was a storekeeper who, upon a certain day ten years ago, had been on his front porch sorting apples in a barrel when two gun-blazing hellions roared by on stolen horses with one toting a bulging canvas sack bearing the stencilled initials S.R.W.B., San Rafael Westland Bank.

The storekeeper had taken part in the subsequent laying to rest in the Strangers' Ground at the cemetery of the mortal remains of one Lucas McCoy and would gladly perform the same civic services for the husky man in denim shirt and moleskin pants cluttering up his sidewalk now, given half an opportunity. But Struther Cady just smiled. For anybody accustomed to being cursed like a dog from daylight to dusk over many years, hearing yourself being labelled 'vermin' by gentlefolk was almost like a caress.

The bunch on the Ten Bar porch acted startled when the ex-con suddenly stepped down off the walk and crossed the street, making directly towards them. They parted cravenly and he smiled and went through to the bar.

'Beer,' he ordered.

The bartender, large, rotund and sombre gave him stare for stare in the congealing silence.

'They don't pay me enough to serve the likes of you.'

A rumble of approval swept the bar-room and, glancing at the mirror, Cady met the hostile glare of twenty pairs of eyes.

He turned and leaned his back against the mahogany edge as curious heads appeared above the batwings.

'Don't blame you for a minute, folks,' he stated amiably. 'If I were you, I wouldn't just not serve me, I'd kick me right out on my Protestant ass.'

He held up his hands for silence as the muttering erupted again.

'I'd just like you to know that I did the crime and I did my time – hard. Man! But was it ever hard. But I had it comin'. And if one thing the slammer offers

35

a man, it's all the time in the world to reflect. By the time I was through reflectin' I knew that when I got out I still wasn't goin' to feel like I'd paid my full debt to society. You know? Not one hundred per cent.' He spread his hands. 'That's why I'm here. Come back to say I'm sorry personal. Hey, I won't blame anybody who tells me to go straight to hell. But I'm a free man now and I'm as free to tell you how I feel just as you folks are free to show me the gate if you feel you gotta.'

It was silent as he turned to slap the bar.

'Another time mebbe, pal,' he told the barman. He was heading for the doors when a voice sounded from the staircase landing above the silent room.

'Why not give the man a drink, Al?' The voice was smooth and cultivated. Glancing upwards, Cady saw that the speaker was a smoothly virile-looking character who was leaning gracefully on the balustrade with a pretty young woman at his side. The fellow threw him a casual gesture and continued: 'We're all law-abiding citizens here, and as such we abide by the law that says when a man has done his time, it's over. He's entitled to a fresh start on level terms with his fellow man. Leastways that is the way I've always seen it, correct me if I'm wrong.'

Glancing round the room Cady could see the man's words taking effect. He realized he was a commanding sort of fellow and his quiet words certainly seemed to carry weight. He heard a thump behind him, swung to see that a glass and bottle of beer had been set up on the counter.

He grinned at the sombre barkeep and spun a

dollar on to the bar. He poured his drink and held the glass aloft to the man on the landing.

'Much obliged, mister.' He ventured a cheeky grin. 'Can't say I recall you from when I was here last.'

Several drinkers muttered curses but it didn't amount to anything. The well-dressed man with the dimple in his chin and an impressive head of tight golden curls flashed the ex-con a sunny smile.

'My name's Santone, Emile Santone.'

'Again, much obliged, Mr Santone. And the young lady?'

Santone took the 'young lady's' hand and gave it a squeeze.

'Trina,' he said formally, 'Mr Struther Cady. Cady, meet Miss Trina Tillerman.'

Cady spluttered in his beer.

'Tillerman?' he couldn't help gasping in surprise. For if ever there was one, that was a name from the past with a real bite to it!

CHAPTER 3

THE VIOLENT ONES

'What do you see in him, honey?'

'He's handsome, well-educated and a real man. But most important, he loves me.'

'And what—?'

'No. No more "and what's", Father. That's all you need to know despite what mother may have told you.'

Tillerman glared at his daughter. Once, that would have been sufficient to intimidate her; the scowl had always been his last resort. Times had plainly changed. She'd grown up and she was defending something important to her. He snapped his fingers and the waitress arrived at their table smartly.

'I'll have something to go in this coffee,' he said.

'Something, sir?'

'Whiskey.'

'But—'

'Whiskey!'

The girl hurried off. Trina Tillerman, a twenty-year-younger version of her mother, linked her fingers beneath her chin and smiled at her father across the table.

'Well, at least you intimidated her, Father. So, why don't you tell me about all those people you shot at Black Bluff?'

His scowl was black but Tillerman knew she was winning this set piece hands down. There were two reasons for this. One, she had grown up since he last saw her. And two, she had always been his weakness, so much so that he sensed he would rather see her betrothed to a Comanche rain-dancer with ornamental bones through his nose than ever be at odds with her.

If he really needed to have a beautiful and educated female to fight with there was always his wife.

'All I did at Black Bluff was buy you this,' he growled producing the package. It was a set of pure gold earrings. She blushed and kissed him and they were back on the old easy footing they'd enjoyed when they parted. But watching her walk away from him on the street, young, spirited and full of life, Tillerman knew it was anything but over, but rather just beginning.

He went searching for the man whom his wife insisted would make a totally unsuitable husband for anyone, much more their daughter.

The meeting between them began badly and went downhill from there. Diplomacy had never been one of Tillerman's attributes, while Emile Santone was proving a far more formidable personality than Sam had anticipated. His first impressions of his daughter's heart-interest had been clear enough. Too flashy, too sure of himself, a dude with immaculate manners which seemed strangely at odds with shoulders as broad as Tillerman's own; that was Trina's beau. And when you seasoned these qualities with a suave charm and reckless handsomeness, they spelled out all too clearly to the former king of Tadpole Ranch just one thing – fortune-hunter!

Characteristically he saw no good reason why, after several minutes of verbal thrust and parry here in the comfortable surrounds of the Hotel Paramount's back parlour, he should not make his feelings known. It was the Tillerman way. You called a spade a spade, or a ladies'-man-cum-goldigging-lounge-lizard on the make – exactly that.

Unfazed as he relaxed with one well-tailored elbow resting on a polished rosewood cutlery cabinet, Emile Santone listened to himself being described as a 'snaky fortune-hunter' with a small smug smile, the sort of look an adult might adopt while waiting out the tantrum of a wayward child.

But Santone was not Tillerman's only audience. Long before the two men had kept their prearranged appointment to meet for a 'discussion' on matters of mutual interest, the word had got out about what was in the air.

During his whirlwind three weeks in the county capital, Santone had assumed a position of high visibility and some status. That was due less to his skills

40

with the pasteboards, or the general effect he was having on the female population of San Rafael, than to his almost immediate involvement with Trina Tillerman – just turned sweet eighteen in contrast to the newcomer's fortyish look.

It was no secret that Caroline Tillerman had reacted badly to this scenario straight from every doting mother's nightmare, and it didn't surprise anyone when Big Sam had shown up out at the spread from nowhere soon after. There was no prize for guessing who or what had brought him back to those 15,000 prime acres he'd once called home.

There was a dumb-waiter aperture in the rear wall of the dining-room which gave on to the galley, and there a cluster of men, women and one pot boy were clustered, listening to every word and laying bets on how long it might be before Tillerman's famous temper erupted and the shouting began.

This interest was not confined just to the hotel.

Close by outside on the streets evening strollers and saloon topers alike found excuses to loiter along the plankwalks and porches, smoking, taking the night air and speculating on just how the showdown might go.

Tillerman was still very much a prominent figure in San Rafael life even if he had not lived there for some time. He invariably attracted attention on visits here which was not the same thing as attracting general admiration. The records showed that Big Sam had won far more fights than he'd lost over the years; and there was always the bank-robbery episode to ensure that he was viewed as some kind of hero to

41

many a citizen.

None the less, although his adversary tonight was something of an unknown quantity, the general impression Emile Santone conveyed to the sharp observer, was that beneath his almost too smooth exterior lurked a man moulded from far tougher stuff than chin-dimples, sparkling teeth and glossy blond curls might indicate.

But while Tillerman was sporting his most intimidating persona by this time, Santone still appeared affable and unflappable as he smilingly shook his head.

'Ah, Tillerman, you're a big disappointment to me, that's all I can say. I mean – real big. To hear Trina talk about you, I was expecting to meet somebody special. You know: "My daddy the world-beater"? But what do I find? Just another broken-winded old fuddy-duddy pappy who wants to keep baby daughter all to himself so no evil-minded lecher can come along and hustle her away to the altar so he can get his meathooks into daddy's cash account. What a letdown!'

Tillerman stood in pulsing silence, eyes unblinking, powerful arms folded across an arching chest. He appeared completely unimpressed as the seconds ticked by, yet that was far from the case.

Santone had balls.

He had not expected this. Rather, he'd hoped this troublemaking suitor might simply fold as most men of his breed did when confronted by someone of his size and importance when they showed ready to stand up and call a spade a spade.

And drawing now from the well of human experience he'd acquired over the years, Tillerman was beginning to sense, without having proof of it yet, that Santone was a seasoned and maybe even a hardened fortune-hunter, a man very much on the make who had been round the traps in his time. He reckoned this one knew how many beans made five. That he could most likely calculate to within the dollar just how much marriage to the daughter of Samuel and Caroline Tillerman's only child might be expected to net a successful suitor.

The slick-smiling, wavy-haired son of a bitch!

But before he would allow himself go too far down that track, Tillerman reined himself in. Summoning his self-discipline, he sucked in several calming breaths and forced himself to focus on the end result, not the obstacles he might encounter along the way.

What he wanted out of this parley, of course, was to see the relationship broken off, Trina back home with her mother and Santone gone. And in situations like that you could often get more with sugar than salt.

'Emile,' he said through locked teeth. 'Er, don't mind if I call you Emile, do you?'

'That's my name . . . Sam.'

Tillerman's knuckles tingled. He ignored them.

'Emile, would you like to tell me your intentions towards my daughter?'

'I mean to marry her, of course.'

Tillerman had to clear his throat. Twice.

'Kind of sudden, wouldn't you say?' he rasped.

'Not as sudden as you and Caroline, eh? Proposed the night after you first met, so I'm told. Whew! Just as well I wasn't Caroline's pappy then. It would have been horsewhip time, for sure.'

'How the hell old are you?' Self-control was slipping again.

'Thirty-seven.'

'Nineteen years my daughter's senior!'

'And twelve years your junior, Sam.' Santone suddenly ceased smiling. He slid off the bureau and moved around on the soft-pile carpet on the balls of his feet like a prizefighter.

'All right, why don't we cut the bull and get down to cases, Tillerman. When Trina and I met we fell for each other on sight; her mother threw a fit. She sent for you and now you're here to try and bust us up. Isn't that a pretty good evaluation of the situation?'

'Well, I . . . er. . . .'

'I'll take that as a yes.'

Santone halted before him. The younger man was a couple of inches shorter but extra wide of shoulder and slender of waist. Tillerman's customary feeling of physical superiority was plainly being challenged. He stretched himself up to full height and thrust out his chin, but had to admit that the clean-shaven cleft jaw before him was every bit as formidable as his own.

'OK,' Santone continued, gently punching his right fist into his left palm. 'That's your situation. And to cut through all this, here's mine. I plan to marry your daughter just as soon as she says yes and nothing you can throw at me can stop me.' He spread his hands, no pearly teeth visible now. 'How is that for straight, Big Sam?'

'How many times have you been married?'

'You're wasting both our time, big man.'

'How many times have you been behind bars, you slippery, heel-clicking gigolo?'

'Too bad you're such a predictable, fire-snorting hick, Tillerman,' Santone said, turning for the door. 'I like your style, and we could have hit it off just fine if you weren't a bit-champing and sour-bellied old bronc—'

'Where do you think you're going?'

Out in the kitchen, eyes rolled and breaths sucked in to hear that note in Tillerman's voice. The eaves-droppers didn't dare take a peek. But had they done so they would have seen Santone halt with his back to the bigger man, jaw muscles tightening and fists clenched tight as he stared straight ahead at the doors.

'Out is where, Tillerman,' he replied softly. 'I'd just hate to think you'd be fool enough to try and stop me.'

'You're not quitting this room until we've settled about you and my daughter, you fortune-hunting son of a bitch.'

Santone turned smoothly and very fast. Outside somewhere a dry leaf skittered along the boardwalk and a tethered mule, shifting its weight nervously, jangled its harness. Tillerman's words hung in the air of the quiet room, a challenge issued and a line drawn.

'A man can call me that once but never twice, Tillerman. Take it back.'

'No chance.'

Now the younger man whirled.

'Then go straight to hell!' He charged.

Tillerman threw the first punch. It was a full-powered overhanded right and quicker than a gazelle trying to jump into bed before it got dark after dousing the light.

The fact that the punch landed flush on the target of Santone's jaw was rewarding. But the result was anything but. Santone blinked but didn't go down. Nor did he take a backward step. What he did was weave low and put his shoulder behind a blurring left fist that pistoned wrist-deep into Tillerman's rocky mid-section and damn near put him down.

Big Sam still didn't know exactly who this man with designs on his daughter might prove to be. But forced to back up a step and throw up his guard, he was getting a pretty clear notion of what he was, namely a genuine fighter and teak-tough, spit-and-polish style notwithstanding.

He backed up with hands dropping low as though hurt more than he really was. Santone was suckered in. He let fly with a haymaker. Tillerman blocked with his left forearm and connected with a jolting right to the point which travelled no further than six inches yet landed with the impact of a pile-driver.

Wearing an expression of almost comic astonishment, Santone hit the carpet hard.

Yet before Tillerman could follow up with a lashing kick the other rolled with catlike agility to dive beneath a big teak dining-table. He popped up on the other side, smoothing down his hair with both hands, still managing to grin despite a tiny rivulet of

46

crimson trickling from the corner of his mouth.

'For a creaky old man, you pack a tolerable wallop, Tillerman.'

Tillerman wasn't talking. Light-footed he circled the table with big fists cocked, eyebrows hooked upwards and jaw tucked in, a prizefighter moving in for the knockout before the round-end bell could ring.

He walked into a straight left he didn't even see coming. The blow knocked him off balance and before he could recover Santone came swarming in, throwing them from all angles, raking to the mid-section, then switching to the head with a combination left and right then back to the solar plexus again.

Tillerman got serious.

In one oiled motion he snatched up one of the Paramount's better chairs and broke it across the head and shoulders of his adversary, who gave at the knees.

'Anything goes, eh, Tillerman? Well try this for size, buffalo man!'

Santone's flashing right boot caught him in the groin and put him down in white-hot agony.

'Bastard!' Tillerman raged, ducking a second kick and making it up to one knee. His face was grey and his eyes bugged from the pain with big veins sticking out of his forehead. 'You'll keep away from our little girl or I'll bust every bone in your crummy body.'

'That is stand-up talk, big man,' Santone panted, circling him like a catamount. 'But you're not standing and I am. Seen this trick before, big shot?'

Santone spun like an acrobat on one foot then lashed out with a truly venomous kick with the other – an explosive attack trick picked up from a kung fu master in Texas. The boot disarrayed Tillerman's hair but didn't even graze his scalp. Santone was counting on making full contact and maybe ending then and there the brawl which by now had attracted dozens of onlookers with the crash and smash of tumbling furniture.

He didn't regain his equilibrium quickly enough.

Tillerman came up off the floor and caught him with a driving shoulder under the armpit. Locked together, they crashed into a glass-fronted cake-cupboard, rolling in a cascade of shattered glass, punching, kicking and gouging like a couple of dock brawlers fuelled up on cheap booze and bad temper.

Tillerman no longer looked invincible and Santone was just a staggering shadow of his debonair self as they clambered erect again over by the servery. A moment's staggering, hard-breathing hesitation, then they came together again with a crash like a pair of range bulls to stand toe to toe for a handful of truly brutal seconds of pure violence until something simply had to give.

It was Santone.

Spitting blood and with breath rasping in his lungs, the younger man took a whistling fist flush to the jaw and crashed back into the wall. As he bounced off it, Tillerman was balancing on the soles of his feet and waiting for him. The next punch knocked Santone down.

Tillerman's vicious kick missed its target when

Santone somehow slipped between his legs to bob up behind him, an incredible recovery. As Tillerman whirled with a curse a door crashed open in back of his adversary. Quicker than the eye could follow, Santone dived a hand inside his jacket to whip out a .38 as he spun on dancing feet to confront the fresh trouble.

Slowly the weapon came down as the combatants stared into the sober, moustached features of Sheriff Nate Poole.

'Did you see that, Nate?' Tillerman croaked, sleeving a bloodied mouth and clutching at his side where a severe stitch was biting hard. 'The way he just came clear? Ever see anybody but a dirty owlhoot who could draw iron that . . . ?'

'He started it, Sheriff,' gasped Santone, slipping his piece away. 'He—'

'And I'll finish it,' broke in a glowering Poole, glancing in disgust at the widespread wreckage. 'Hand over your weapons and come with me, you are both under arrest.'

'But, Nate—' was as far as a genuinely shocked Big Sam was allowed to get.

'You're up for fines and damages already, Sam,' barked one of Tillerman's few genuine friends in San Rafael. 'One more word I'll have you for riot, affray and creating alarm and panic amongst the citizenry.'

Wordless, seething and impotent, the brawlers traded murderous glares as they handed over their guns.

Santone sat on his cell bunk holding a pocket-mirror

49

borrowed from the sheriff, critically inspecting the damage to his face, most of which appeared to be superficial. Across the way occupying the opposite cell of the San Rafael city jailhouse, Tillerman paced like a caged animal, all muscle and heavy breathing. He also had sustained a welter of visible damage but appeared indifferent to skinned knuckles, a gashed eye, swollen mouth and a dozen assorted bruises and scrapes as he cracked his big bony knuckles and kept stabbing scorching glances over his shoulder at his 'good pard' the sheriff.

Seated at his neat desk, pen in hand and pipe going nicely, Nate Poole, sober in dark brown shirt, leather vest and string-tie with moustache neatly brushed, was an island of calm beneath his overhead light as he methodically listed charges and damages, then completed a report on the Paramount incident in a buckskin-bound ledger.

The prisoners were still not permitted to speak. This was their cooling-off period and the sheriff was determined they observe it to the letter.

A lawman of the old school was Nate Poole, quietly spoken, authoritative, fair-minded and more than capable of enforcing the law in a rugged cattle-town boasting over 3,000 permanent citizens.

Under his steady hand San Rafael had not witnessed a single major crime since the robbery of the Westland Bank years earlier. Although one of the two-man bandit gang had been killed, and the other was just out of prison after serving a long stretch, the fact that the Westland's $20,000 had never been recovered remained the one significant blot on an otherwise impeccable lawman's career. But if that long-ago incident bothered Nate Poole – or anything else for that matter – it never showed. Any more than did any suggestion of concern that he now found himself in the process of charging a man he liked better than anyone else in the county in Sam Tillerman.

Unflappable? Nate Poole could write a book on it.

At last he was through, by which time Tillerman had stopped pacing to torch up a fat cigar. A cooler Emile Santone was dressing his fine blond curls with a pocket-comb with a mother-of-pearl handle.

'All right,' said the law, turning his swivel-chair to face the cells. He raised one boot to a footstool and linked lean fingers over a small, comfortable paunch. 'You first, Santone.'

'Shouldn't that be "Mister" Santone, Sheriff?' the man fired back. 'That's who I was yesterday.'

'That was before I received this.' The lawman used his pipestem to tap a letter in his paper tray. 'Further information on your background in Nevada which I told you I was seeking on behalf of Mrs Caroline Tillerman. I have to tell you not all of it is good, mister, not good at all.'

'Just how bad is it, Nate?' Tillerman demanded. 'I mean, this is what all this is about, as you damn well know even if you pretend otherwise. It's all about this peckerhead and his total unsuitability to pay court to our daughter—'

'We're discussing the brawl,' Poole cut in, ' and I gave Santone the floor. So pipe down and sit down, Sam. I won't tell you again.'

Tillerman damn near bit through his cheroot. Yet he did as ordered, leaving Santone to furnish a reasonably accurate summary of events leading up to the brawl at the hotel.

When the man was through, Poole just grunted, nodded to Tillerman. His turn at last.

Being Tillerman he overstated his case despite the sheriff's attempts to achieve brevity, integrity and clarity. Yet he was almost through when the sounds of a rig drawing up outside were heard, followed by swift, light footsteps crossing the porch. Moments later Trina Tillerman was standing before the desk wearing a divided skirt and denim shirt, hands on hips, hat hanging down her back by the throat-strap, the very picture of outrage.

'Father!' she panted. 'So it's true what I heard! How could you!'

It didn't get any better from that unpromising beginning. No matter how hard Big Sam tried to explain, Trina remained convinced beyond reason, logic or his heated protests that it was all his fault. That he had returned home specifically to break them up, had sought out the man of her choice and in 'typical Sam Tillerman fashion', as she scathingly phrased it, tried to beat up the man she loved. She even seemed waspishly pleased to note that her 'invincible' father looked like anything but a winner right now.

'I have never been so disgusted and humiliated in my entire life, Father,' she summarized tearfully, clutching a grinning Santone's hand through the bars of his cell. 'You belong in the Dark Ages. You are

. . . antediluvian! As for you, Sheriff Poole – father's great friend – are you going to release Emile or shall I wake up Judge Turnbull and force you to do so?'

Poole rose and took his keyring down from the wall hook.

'They're both free to leave, Trina. They weren't so much in custody as locked up while they cooled down.'

Poole moved forward to halt between the cells.

'I fully understand the causes of tonight's trouble, you fellows, but that is no concern of mine. This office tries not to interfere in personal matters other than when they impinge on the law. I'm not going to tell you how to sort this out, mainly because I don't know all the ins and outs, and because it's none of my business really. But I'm telling you to your faces – settle things sensibly and not like a couple of tanked-up cowboys in town on a toot. You'll be fined ten dollars apiece in the morning and the Paramount will give me a detailed cost-accounting of damages which you'll meet between you. Other than that, I don't want to hear another word more of this affair and I won't tolerate any repetition. Savvy?'

Two heads nodded.

Moments later they were free. Big Sam insisted on hugging his daughter even though a stiff-backed Trina made no response. He sighed as he released her. As attractive as her mother but far too much like Caroline for her own good; that was his assessment of this newly matured and suddenly rebellious eight-een-year-old. She was also assertive, cantankerous, single-minded and over-talkative in his private opinion. Was it any wonder he had kissed goodbye a $250,000 cattle empire in return for his freedom from this petticoat tyranny?

Suddenly he found himself staring down at an outstretched hand.

'No hard feelings, Tillerman?' Santone proffered.

'What?'

'Oh, Emile, that's such a fine gesture,' gushed Trina, hanging on to the man's muscular arm. 'After what Father did to your face.' Then she scowled. 'Well, Father, what are you waiting for?'

'I'm not shaking hands with any gun-toting, eye-gouging, heel-clicking gold-digger who Nate Poole's got paper on, girl,' Tillerman stated emphatically.

'Hey, don't be a sore loser, Sam,' Santone said with that infuriating smile. 'We're just a pair of mossyhorns, you and me. We see something we don't like, and we charge. But no point in going on with it, especially under the circumstances.'

'Which are?' Tillerman's tone was ominous.

Santone slipped an arm about the girl's slim waist and squeezed.

'Trina and me, of course. We're in love and mean to stay that way. You know, wedding-bells, pitter-patter of little feet. The whole symphony.'

'Easy now, Sam,' cautioned Poole, reading the warning signs in Tillerman's writhing jaw muscles and glittering glare.

But Tillerman was under control, even if madder than he'd been in years. 'Caroline's mother asked me to visit because she considered our daughter was involved with an unsuitable type,' he said through clenched teeth. 'Now I've met you I feel the same way. In spades. We're going to fight this all the way, mister, and you might as well both know that if you ever got to walk down the aisle together we'd cut Trina off without one thin dime. So how do you like those apples, Goldilocks?'

'Come along, Emile,' Trina said furiously, tugging the man by the hand. 'I'm not standing for any more of this. I shall see you at the ranch, Father, you and Mother. There's a lot I wish to say to both of you that a young lady should not be heard saying in public.'

'You're making a big mistake, Sam,' Santone drawled as they made for the door. 'We could be pals. You know, like you and the sheriff?'

'Not one thin dime, pilgrim.'

Santone halted in the doorway. 'Want a bit of good old-fashioned advice?'

'Not from you, I don't.'

'Old cowboy saying: "Always carry more than one rope. Who knows? One day you might run across more than one rope can handle." See you soon . . . Dad.'

Then they were gone.

Tillerman stood staring after them as though his boots were nailed to the floorboards. The sheriff crossed to the desk and produced a bottle and two glasses. He held them up under the light, smiling ruefully.

'The joys of parenthood, Sam.'

'Do me a big favour, Nate.'
'What's that?'
'Shut up, and pour.'

CHAPTER 4

TILLERMAN'S WAY

The unfriendly barkeep accepted his silver this time around, and the drinker at the bar didn't immediately move off when Struther Cady leaned an elbow on the counter at his side.

Progress! the ex-con mused wryly. Nothing to get excited about maybe, but he was definitely making some kind of headway.

And listening to the conversation reaching him in waves from the tables, the gambling layouts and dance-floor where skimpily clad girls danced desultorily with slim riders in big hats and spurs, the ex-bandit-cum-jailbird realized he mainly had Big Sam Tillerman, his old nemesis, to thank for this.

All the talk today was of that spectacularly noisy ruckus at the hotel between Tillerman and Santone. This had immediately drawn the focus off Cady and placed it someplace else, which suited him just fine.

Seemed to him that all San Rafael had been waiting on tenterhooks for Tillerman to return and deal with the Trina–Santone romance, which the mother seemed to find so abhorrent. Now he was back there had been a rafter-shaking donnybrook and, according to some eye-witnesses, Santone had given about as good as he got, which might well be the first time on record Big Sam had started a fight and not been able to finish it.

Inwardly, Struther Cady was standing up and applauding, whistling and stamping both boots in appreciation of Santone's performance. Outwardly however, he offered no comment even when the barfly at his side started in about the dust-up.

Cady was only relieved that Tillerman had come out of the clash without being seriously hurt or killed.

Funny how a man could feel that way about a man whose guts he would cheerfully feed to the dogs.

Cady hated Tillerman.

But hating someone and wanting them dead were not necessarily the same thing. For, by the careless vagaries of fortune and destiny, the lives of the lethal ex-con and the big man were inexorably linked. Cady had robbed a bank, Tillerman had led the manhunt after himself and McCoy, who'd perished leaving the whereabouts of the $20,000 – Cady's $20,000 as he saw it – unknown.

But Cady meant to know. That was the reason he was back. Maybe a secondary ambition would be to put a .44 slug through Tillerman's stinking heart. But the prime goal and the holy grail was the big *dinero*.

One way or another, sooner or later, Cady meant

to find a way to spend time with Tillerman and if possible get to ingratiate himself with the big man before asking a king-sized favour of a man who did not do favours. This would be as formidable a challenge as this hardcase had ever set himself, as things stood. But he told himself he must succeed without jeopardizing whatever slim chances of success he might have by any loose talk.

Eventually the barfly realized he wasn't getting anyplace on the Big Sam topic, seemingly only then belatedly to realize whom he was talking to.

'Hey, you're that crook they've all been talkin' about, ain't you?' he slurred. 'The one what held up the bank way back?'

'Guess I am, pard.' Cady sipped his beer. He was drinking sparingly. A man needed to keep his wits about him in this man's town. This was no post-penitentiary summer vacation for Struther Cady. No way.

'What'dja do with it?'

'Huh?' Cady grunted, as if he didn't know.

The man leaned closer confidentially. His breath was a knee-weakening combination of sour booze, halitosis and stale tobacco blended aromatically with an overripe body odour that any camel would be proud of.

'The loot, of course. The stash, the cash, the twenty grand they never found. Nobody's been talkin' about nothin' else since you showed, Cady. What beats me though is why nobody seems to think you've come back for it. Why, every time I mention the big *dinero*, they just shake their heads and say it's gone. How can twenty thousand dollars just disappear thataway?'

'Simple enough. My buddy had it when we split up, he croaked and they never found it.'

Cady's mouth cut down at the corners with bitter recollection. 'All I got out of the caper was some rough handling by Sam Tillerman, a thirty-minute trial and ten years on the rockpile.'

'And you're sore as a boil about it, ain't you? C'mon, admit it. I can tell. Risk your neck for twenty thousand, money disappears, buddy dies, ten years inside. Who wouldn't be sore?'

But the lush was talking to himself as Cady threaded his way off between the tables. He had things on his mind. Yet that didn't stop him saluting a man here, pausing for a word with another there *en route*. He was working overtime every minute he was in San Rafael, slogging hard at the challenge of forcing the place to get used to him, accepting him despite the baggage of the past he carried. And all for a purpose, of course. In reality, Cady didn't give one rap if the entire county hated him for eternity providing he could ingratiate himself here sufficiently just to get by unimpeded while he went about the serious work of winning Tillerman's confidence. That was a mammoth task by itself without having to deal with hostile towners on the side.

Sam was his man.

So he was watching out for the big man as he went prowling the full length of the long main street, but without success. Yet despite the importance and urgency of his search, failure seemed scarcely to matter for the moment. For right at that moment, Struther Cady was a man starved of life, colour, excitement and all the wonderful hurly-burly of regular existence outside prison walls after ten lost years. He realized only now that, so single-minded had he been in kicking the rockyard dust of the penitentiary off his prison-issue boots and making it back to the scene of the crime, that he had barely afforded himself a moment just to soak it all up again . . . this sweet thing called freedom.

Kelly Street, San Rafael, was as good a place to celebrate a return to real life as a man might find in the whole Territory.

He strolled past roaring beer-joints, checked out the mysterious items in the drugstore windows and stood unconsciously tapping his foot to the badly played yet exhilarating piano music thumping out of a dance-parlour that was lit up like Saturday night in Denver.

Drunks and young couples, cowboys in chaps and zigzagging old hobos crowded the walks, and scarce anyone pointed him out or yelled 'jailbird!' any more. Not liking or trusting him, but getting to accept him. That was progress. Approaching the penny arcade garishly illuminated by candles in multicoloured glass globes, he ducked a door-leaner's flipped cigarette butt and was jostled by an old man in a Civil War greatcoat toting wine bottles in a huge paper sack.

He inhaled perfume and absorbed music and voices, the drumbeat of heels on planking, the hoarse shouts of cowboys and drunks. He actually halted before the plain pink building set a little back from the street with a red light burning above the recessed doorway where a half-dressed woman smoking a cigarette was visible just inside, where all was red plush and subdued lighting. He felt a stirring in his groin and was wondering if finding Tillerman mightn't well wait until tomorrow, when an elbow nudged him in the back. He turned to see Emile Santone with a girl on his arm winking back at him over his shoulder as he sauntered by. Santone, whom he'd seen around town more than most due to the fact that neither of them seemed handicapped by an honest job of work at the moment, always acted friendly and was doing so now, flashing a big grin as his pretty companion also turned to look back at him.

Suddenly something rang. Santone was keeping company with Tillerman's daughter!

'Hey, Emile!' he called, starting after the couple. 'Wait up.'

They let him tag along for a spell; just three people out enjoying themselves on the street at night. But not everyone in San Rafael tonight would see it that way.

Tillerman studied his glass. 'Good liquor, Nate. But then you never kept any other kind. At least that's something that hasn't changed.'

'The law-office bottle and you, old friend. Two things.'

'Somehow that doesn't sound like a compliment.'

'You're still the same old mossyhorn you always were, Sam,' declared the sheriff, pouring another then stoppering the bottle with an air of finality.

They clinked glasses and he went on: 'I'm not sure it was smart of Caroline to send for you, and I'm dead sure it was not anyway smart for you to take Santone on the way you did, like a bull at a gate. If you'll take the advice of a man who's not even married, let alone got a grown-up daughter to deal with – you don't go at problems like this that way. A man has to be more . . . more diplomatic.'

'Diplomatic? I hate that word.'

'Tell me something I don't know.'

Tillerman brooded a little. It was true, what Nate Poole said. He most always dealt with an adversary the same way. First you studied him. You prodded him to see what he was made of and how much he'd take. When you knew, you grabbed him and started shaking, and you kept on shaking until he fell apart. That was Tillerman's way. Most often it worked, but not always.

He raised his hands and dropped them in a gesture of resignation.

'All right, Nate, what's a man to do in a situation like this anyway?'

'Go easy, is what.'

'Go easy? Trina's talking marriage with this joker, Caroline is climbing the walls, and I've got an angry redhead and a big cattle deal up north that won't wait. How much time is there?'

'You asked me, old friend.'

Tillerman went to the jailhouse door which stood open to the night. San Rafael was bustling as he surveyed it moodily. The odour of frying pork and hot coffee drifted by, reminding him he hadn't eaten in eight hours. Didn't want to either. He was a man with troubles on his mind.

Then he remembered. He whirled sharply.

'Santone—'

'Wondered when you'd remember.' The lawman drew a letter from a pile of papers on his desk, tapped it on his thumbnail. 'This puts me in a bit of a quandary, I don't mind telling you. Don't see how it's going to help this situation you've stirred up, one way or another. . . .'

'For Pete's sake don't be an old woman, man. What have you got on him?'

Poole opened the letter and glanced at the contents.

'A further record search in Nevada reveals that Santone killed a man in a gunfight – a fair duel by all accounts. He was charged with trading in spurious stocks and bonds and forced to pay a one-thousand-dollar fine and a further two thousand compensation in order to avoid going to prison. He is reputedly wanted on an undisclosed charge in Hud County and is regarded as a person of questionable character by the City Marshal of Durango. . . .'

'In other words, he's nothing but a dirty, low-down crook.'

'Or just another huckster on the make. Depends on your interpretation I guess, Sam.'

'Anything else?'

'That's all on Santone.'

'You're investigating someone else?'

'Right.' Poole rose and both men went out on to the porch, where the evening air was cool and refreshing, where life pulsed buoyantly through San

Rafael. The lawman dropped into a rocker with his pipe, digging into his shirt pocket for tobacco. 'I've been in contact with the warden of Duell Basin Penitentiary concerning another man of interest to you. Cady.'

'Damn right I'm interested. What's the pen say about him?'

'Did his time straight and hard. Kept to himself mostly. Warden sounds almost impressed. Suggests Cady entered prison as a tough young punk with chips on both shoulders and came out a man with grit in his gizzard.'

'Is that supposed to impress us?'

'I'm not looking to be impressed, just trying to get a line on what brought him back.' Poole paused. 'Can't help figuring it's got to be connected with the bank job, of course. Which in turn means something to do with the missing money.'

Sam Tillerman nodded his big head slowly as he watched little brown bats whirling against the moon. Naturally that self-same thought had crossed his mind the first moment he came face to face with wang-and-rawhide Struther Cady ten years on.

A man was not likely to forget about $20,000 after taking such risks to steal it before losing contact with it for ten years.

But lost it certainly had been.

The day of the hold-up, when badly wounded Lucas McCoy and Struther Cady blasted their way clear of town to reach Black Rock out along the Dreamer's Mountain trail, with a town posse raging in hot pursuit, Cady had been the one toting the

65

bank-bag into which they'd stuffed the entire contents of the vaults.

The pair dropped from sight briefly amongst the rocks to consider their desperate situation. When McCoy reappeared to go hammering east at the gallop, he was alone. Despite his wounds, Cady stood the possemen off for several hours before blood-loss brought on his collapse and capture.

When at last the frantic searchers found the bank-sack at the rock it was empty; Cady denied there'd ever been any money, then clammed up.

The concentrated search of the sprawling Two Mile Rock region which followed occupied days during which time trenches were dug, deadfalls ripped to pieces and rocks blasted with dynamite in an increasingly frenzied attempt to locate the hiding-place of the big twenty.

It was realized only then that McCoy had taken the booty – and Tillerman had gone off after him.

When a wounded Tillerman eventually returned from snow-covered Dreamer's Mountain with McCoy's corpse and not one centavo of the Westland cash, the madness began.

Tillerman could only offer a sketchy account of the terrain he'd covered on the mountain. The drifts were ten feet deep in places up there but that didn't prevent dozens of eager fortune-hunters rushing out to begin the search for the Westland dollars.

It was a month before the bank officially conceded that the money was most likely unrecoverable, another two years before citizens, treasure-hunters and others finnally stopped travelling out to the mountain every weekend to continue the search.

Plainly Cady had been too clever for them, and in time even Sheriff Poole, the bank president and San Rafael itself recovered from the loss and the whole sorry affair gradually faded into the past.

It had stayed there until a gaunt ex-con with a jail-house close-crop and rock-breaker's calluses on his palms thick enough to line brake-shoes with showed up on a played-out horse a decade on.

Tillerman felt he could have done without Cady right now, yet could not deny his own curiosity about the man, particularly when the sheriff revealed that his own thoughts were centred on the money.

'Are you thinking what I'm thinking, Nate?' he asked abruptly.

'Which is?'

'That Cady's come back to recover the loot McCoy hid away that day?'

'Those honorable if pretty heavy-handed gentle-men who run Duell Basin pen seem to think other-wise, Sam,' was Poole's wry response.

'Meaning?'

'Meaning . . . they beat the living crap out of him for three months after he arrived, trying to get him to 'fess up about the cache. After Cady landed in the infirmary three times with injuries thus received, still without revealing a word, they were convinced they were wrong. I'm convinced myself, now more than ever.'

'Why?'

'Cady's been here for days, wandering out, trying

to make friends, making his dough spin out. If he knew where the money was on the mountain he'd have come, got it and vanished without anyone even knowing he was around. Make sense to you?'

But suddenly Tillerman's attention was diverted. Approaching from the direction of the general store and the City Billiard Parlour, were three people, two men and a woman. They came strolling along together, the couple arm-in-arm, the second man with his hands thrust deep into his pockets and nodding his close-cropped skull as the trio passed beneath a streetlight.

The other man laughed, and Tillerman recognized the V-shaped torso, the cocky walk and the curly fair head of Emile Santone. He recognized his own daughter last of all. She had blossomed so that he was still not adjusted to the fact that Trina was now a woman.

Poole saw him stiffen, then propel himself out of his rocking-chair.

'Goddamn!' said the sheriff. Then he seized Tillerman by the arm. 'Now go easy, Sam. It's still a free country and folks are entitled to mix with whomever they want, when they want. That is the law.'

Tillerman knew this as well as he did. And he was a man who supported the laws of the United States, had fought for them more than once. But all such considerations went straight out the window on seeing his daughter, his precious girl, promenading down Kelly Street arm-in-arm with a man he was pretty sure was a crook of some description, both of them in the company of a tried and convicted bank robber just let out of the Duell Basin big house.

A father could only take so much.

The scene which unfolded in the bright lamplight before the law office was hardly edifying and might have even bordered on the illegal, yet even so, a resigned and understanding Nate Poole made no move to intervene.

Firstly, Tillerman demanded that Trina bid her escort goodnight and accompany him back to Tadpole for a heart-to-heart with himself and her mother. When the angry girl refused, Santone interjected. This goaded Tillerman into blurting out to all three the background information the sheriff had received concerning Santone's record in Nevada. This seemed to set Santone back some, but when Cady objected Tillerman shoved him and sat him on his backside by the horse trough. At this point, Trina became hysterical. Santone came forward as though to take her by the arm and Tillerman hit the man with a haymaker that dropped him to his knees. Only now did the sheriff start down the steps. But he was not quick enough to prevent a grim-faced Big Sam seizing his protesting daughter by the arm and striding off for the livery.

A couple of minutes later, with a still recovering Emile Santone fiddling with his gun handle and threatening to go after Tillerman, a buggy wheeled from the livery and vanished fast along the Tadpole Ranch trail, leaving a cloud of dust and a swelling bunch of puzzled onlookers in its wake.

'All right, break it up!' barked Poole, waving his

arms to send them on their way. 'And you two,' he warned Cady and Santone, 'I don't want to see your faces until the morning, if then. Vamoose!'

Subsequently the sheriff was accused behind his back of displaying favouritism towards Sam Tillerman. The criticism was justified. Even Poole would admit this but doubted if Big Sam would either appreciate what he'd done or that his intervention might do the man any good in the long run. Nate Poole had a strong hunch his old friend was going to encounter more trouble out at Tadpole than would have been the case had he not intervened on his behalf here in town. Much more.

CHAPTER 5

FACE TO FACE

Sam Tillerman built things to last. The Tadpole ranch house was a prime example. At the end of his and Caroline's first tough couple of years out along the river that gave the spread its name, he shifted from the two-room cabin they'd shared across by Cobb's Crossing and threw up a big house atop an oak-tree hill several miles north, where the river cascaded down out of the high country to wander away leisurely through broadening vistas of green ranchland until it became lost in misty distance to the south.

The house was still young at around twenty years of age, but was built to last a hundred years or longer. It stood with a kind of serene grandeur on the southern slope of the hill overlooking the cattle-studded land, all of which had eventually come under the Tillerman hand as beef prices boomed and the rancher proceeded on his headlong way to making it as the most successful cattleman in the county. In a land of one- and two-room shacks, here was a castle of red stone, heavy logs and great cedar stakes as thick as a man's arm.

Beneath his authoritative hand a high level of efficiency complemented by the principle of a hard day's work for an honest day's pay had become the pattern on the Tadpole. Things had changed little in this direction since Caroline took over, with the result that work went on as systematically as usual come fair weather or foul, good times or bad.

So it was, that to the eye of the solitary horseman who appeared far out along the town trail next morning, the headquarters presented a reassuring picture of business as usual, with the round-up visible in full swing further out, a trio of lean-hipped hands loping across the Magnolia Pasture to the east, the lazy drift of woodsmoke from the house's big red-clay chimney-pots adding the finishing touch of rural tranquility.

Inside, however, it was hell with all the fences down as Tillerman stood like a big shaggy bear tormented by a relay of hounds in the vast front parlour he'd built with his own sweat and which he'd once dominated as thoroughly as Lincoln had Washington until each tall man in his own dramatic way was brought down to the level of lesser men.

Taking the verbal slings and arrows right on the chin, it flashed through Sam's mind that it was common knowledge that Honest Abe had had to endure a waspish, wifely tongue for many a year before evil John Wilkes Booth's gun bequeathed him to the ages in Ford's Theatre.

He wondered whether, given the choice, he would rather face down a nutter with a revolver than two angry women with tongues that bit like rowelled spurs.

'Had I thought for one moment that you might engage Emile Santone in a vulgar common brawl – that this would be your solution to our problem – I would never have contacted you, Sam Tillerman. I could have told the crew to ride into town and beat the man up. I could have taken a horsewhip to him myself, had I thought along those imbecilic lines.'

That was his ex-wife speaking. Who else was capable of selecting and enunciating her thoughts with such waspish clarity?

'That's my style, damnit. A man won't listen to logical reasoning – I soften him up so he will listen. That's how I built and kept this spread in case you've forgotten, Mrs Tillerman.'

And that was Big Sam, the cornered lion too sore even to put a match to the cheroot clenched between big teeth.

'I've never been so ashamed, humiliated and shocked in all my life, Father. I swear I don't know how I'll ever be able to face Emile, or walk down the main street of San Rafael again. How could you?'

Daughter Trina formed the third corner of this warring triangle and, just like her mother, knew all the little tricks and twists calculated to try and make a man feel bad.

But backed into a corner and outnumbered two to one was a situation wherein Tillerman could be at his most ruthless and dangerous.

His forefinger jabbed out accusingly as his daughter dabbed at her pretty eyes and Caroline cast a thirsty eye on the sherry decanter.

'Look, Miss Eighteen, don't try and make me the villain of this circus. It wasn't me who clapped my hot little eye on some seedy crook old enough to be my daddy, then went after him as though I was starving and just heard the supper gong. I wasn't taken in by dimples and pearly teeth and a line as bogus as a hardshell Baptist preacher trying to sell a flock of sodbusters on Jesus. You were the star in that farce. It was you who made yourself the laughing-stock of the whole damned county and ignored your mother's advice and damn near drove her to the bottle!'

At this point, the girl whirled and rushed up the stairs, sobbing and trembling. But this withdrawal did not mean the enemy had been defeated.

'Your own daughter!' accused a white-faced Caroline. 'How could you speak to her that way after last night?'

Hot words sprang to Tillerman's lips but died there. Suddenly he was almost calm as he studied his ex-wife's handsome, spirited face with a kind of detachment. He'd loved her once, and for a long time. Loved her, lusted after her, fought for her, fought with her, enjoyed just about every moment together until the wheels came off the wagon and he finished up almost counting himself lucky to get out of the whole thing for a lousy $100,000 settlement. He should not have come back; that was plain as paint.

Yet in the very moment that he thought this, he

74

knew he had been eager to do so. Had dropped everything, including Marie Elena, to return to Turlock County just as fast as a good rented horse could take him.

Why?

To horn in on some moon-June infatuation of a starry-eyed girl who might well go through another twenty or thirty suitors before she eventually settled down, providing she survived this one?

Hardly.

He'd returned home to see Caroline and the way she looked in the twilight haze or the dawn's early light. Time had plainly dulled the edges of his memory. He had forgotten what drove them apart but she was doing a first-rate job of reminding him afresh. Too good a job, in truth.

He strode for the doors.

'Where do you think you are going, Samuel?'

He didn't pause until he reached the patio where the flowers were in bloom and a housemaid was sweeping off the flagstones.

'You didn't need me, woman. You just snapped your fingers to test if I'd come running. All along, you had your own notions how to handle this deal – how you still will, and how you would've even if I'd succeeded in getting Trina to see sense about that geezer. All right, you've dealt a hand and won the pot. But don't count on next time, because there won't be one.'

She called after him but there was no stopping in the ten paces that carried him out of the courtyard nor the thirty that took him to the stables.

By nature, when he tackled something Tillerman tended to give it all he had, right or wrong. He was like that when he got mad, which was probably more often than it need be. He did mad on the grand scale, and stableboys and yardhands gave him a wide berth now as he saddled his horse, came out of the high-beamed stables at the gallop and sent hens and geese scattering in raucous panic as he tore across the yard, hammered through the gate and set the town trail between the horse's ears.

He didn't look back; that was not his style. Besides, someone had attracted his attention up ahead where the trail snaked out of the hardwood forest for the final straight mile-run to the headquarters. A familiar-looking someone on a tall bay horse, who took off his hat and waved as Tillerman bored towards him.

Santone!

For a moment he was the old Sam Tillerman, bristling and aggressive and ready to go in hard and shove, shake and stomp until something gave – it was the Tillerman way.

But only for a moment. He could rein in his emotions when he wanted. He did so now as he slowed his horse to a lope and the gap between them closed quickly. Every instinct in him might be insisting that Emile Santone was no-account and wildly unsuitable for Trina or any well-reared young lady like her. But Santone was not the real problem here, he convinced himself now. It was the Tillerman women, one too giddy to be able to tell the difference between a nighthawk and a whip-poor-will, the other too full of herself to think anyone but herself capable. Santone was wary as he reined in a short distance uptrail. The right side of the man's jaw was darkly bruised where Tillerman's king-hit had landed. He wore a belt gun today and his free hand rested on walnut butt as with narrowed eyes he waited for the other to speak first.

Tillerman waited until he was drawn abreast before obliging.

'Howdy,' he said.

'Start anything and you'll regret it, Tillerman.'

'I'm not starting anything, mister. I've just finished something one hell of a lot more important than a two-dollar shyster like you.'

He gestured towards the house soaking up the sun below, the movement of his hand flowing and grace-ful.

'On your way, mister. Do your worst, on account I just don't give a damn any more.'

'Throwing in the sponge, Big Sam? I didn't reckon on this.'

'Who cares what you reckon, pipsqueak? You might as well know I'm leaving and I won't be back. Unless, that is, you make me.'

'I don't figure.'

'Do one little thing – one little thing – to hurt my daughter and I'll come back here to the county and I'll break you in two like the dog I reckon you are '

He tipped his hatbrim sardonically, raked with spur and was off, his mount quickly settling to a reaching gallop.

'Well, big man,' Santone murmured with a crooked half-smile. 'All the very best to you too.'

*

For the first time in more than ten years, Struther
Cady drew his polka-dot bandanna up over his face
to rest on the bridge of his nose and conceal his face.
With hatbrim tugged low he was an invisible menace
as he stood motionless behind the stand of pines
watching the horsemen approach.

This was Marble Canyon section, deep in the
Dreamer's Mountain foothills which the ex-con had
been combing with the thoroughness of a prospector
hunting for the big strike. Free range and open land
surrounded the canyon region hereabouts and
people were free to ride its trails or hunt whenever
they had a mind. Cady knew this but wasn't reassured.
Maybe he was overtired; he was certainly mighty tense
due to the fact that he was out here in the boondocks
all alone. But his suspicious eye and tired mind
convinced him that the big rider with the spade beard
and his companion with the sallow complexion and
lantern jaw simply didn't look right somehow. They
wore guns, were well-mounted, and both seemed too
assured and likely-looking to be simple cowpokes,
prospectors or wanderers on the drift.

Two long steps carried him clear of the tree with a
.45 in his fist.

'All right, rein up and step down!' he rapped,
waving the muzzle. 'Pronto!'

Lantern jaw obeyed instantly but spade beard was
way too slow, and his hairy right hand seemed to
move franctionally closer to gun butt as he started in
cussing.

The crash of the shot cut him off mid-cuss, and now the smoking cutter was aimed directly at his face.

'Down! Arms up!' Cady snarled.

The big man swung down in haste, so much so that Cady was forced to step backwards. As he did his heel caught a root. He stumbled with a curse and lantern jaw was on him like a catamount, seizing his gun arm and pistoning a knee into his ribs with brutal force.

Cady saw stars. For a dizzy moment he was tempted to shoot. Then the moment passed and he spun nimbly from the man's grip, came up on one knee and swung his Colt in a vicious arc that terminated against the man's right ear and knocked him sideways, eyes rolling in their sockets.

Jailwise Cady sensed rather than saw the bearded man coming up behind. He somersaulted forwards and sprang to his feet, spun on his heels then swayed smoothly to one side. The charging figure, black-faced with rage, stumbled by and Cady shoved out his foot. He tripped, and Cady kicked him in the head as he went down.

Although spitting blood and seeing double, Cady was still in better shape than anyone else on this lonesome stretch of high trail as he backed up for several paces, breath rasping in his lungs. Both travellers were still on the ground and neither looked any too eager to rise.

'All right, you sons of bitches!' he panted. 'Why are you dogging me – or can I guess?'

Both appeared bewildered. They were. It took time and the presentation of documents from their saddle-bags to prove beyond doubt that the pair were government surveyors *en route* from Katytown to Oak Junction to map out a new stretch of access road through the Buffalo Hills.

If the men expected an apology or even an explanation from their masked assailant, they were destined to be disappointed. But Cady did at least house his six-gun before pointing south, the direction they'd been travelling. They travelled on. Fast.

He dragged the bandanna off his face, turned his head and spat blood. He must ease up some, he advised himself. His search could take weeks, months maybe. If he didn't relax and quit shying at shadows he would be burnt out long before he found the stash.

And he would find it, he reassured himself, gazing around at the landscape which countless treasure seekers had combed and recombed during his long jailhouse years.

They'd found nothing because this was a wide area and they had not known the man who'd hidden the hold-up money.

Cady had likewise found nothing – yet. But he had known his late pard on and off for years, knew how he thought and operated. More than once they'd planted stolen stuff together and had always followed the same general principles. In discussion prior to the robbery they'd laid plans to make their run-out to Dreamer's Mountain; he recalled McCoy actually making some casual reference to vast Marble Canyon and that was the reason he was here, wearing his horse and himself down thin searching for something, anything that might draw his sharper than sharp badman's eye to where bleeding, dying McCoy had stashed the twenty big ones. His big ones, now that McCoy was gone.

Knowing McCoy's style and way of thinking, he would pick out a couple of landmarks – an unsually shaped tree and an odd-coloured rock, then fix on any regular-looking patch of open ground in between – exactly where no gold-hunter would ever consider checking out while he dug and burrowed in all the 'likely' places.

He'd already dug a dozen sizeable holes without result, following this routine. But sooner or later he believed he would find himself sniffing around and suddenly he would see the landmarks that had taken his partner's eye on that fateful day – with Tillerman closing in on him – and it would be all his.

He rolled a cigarette and lighted up. He drew deep and forced a grin. There was lots of time. Nobody understood time better than a man who'd counted ten years of it by the hour.

He whistled and his horse's whicker answered from the woods.

Santone's mount whickered.

The rider reached out and pinched the horse's nostrils together, held his grip as the slow-riding horseman passed below his position amongst the trees. Ten miles out of town, Struther Cady rode tall and arrogant in the saddle whereas in town the man tended to merge into the landscape.

Santone was getting to realize there was far more

to the ex-con than met the eye. This day's absence from town, for instance. When Santone heard Cady had gone riding he'd immediately followed. He guessed the man would head for Dreamer's Mountain and had been proved right.

The mountain stood tall and sombre to the west as Cady faded from sight. Santone's blond brows were drawn tightly together as he felt his pockets for tobacco. He thought: Cady's late partner had lost or stashed a fortune in bank money up there someplace and now Cady was riding around the region. For sentimental reasons?

Santone shook his head. The more he saw and thought about Cady the less thinking-time he seemed to find himself spending on his love life. He'd been doing it hard following a run of washouts upon coming to San Rafael, where a chance meeting with a rich girl had seen himself seriously considering the prospect of marrying for money.

He'd followed up strongly on this inspiration, had done far better, far quicker than he might have hoped. But there were problems and uncertainties associated with the Tillermans – and that factor certainly didn't cause his outlaw heart to kick the way it did whenever he found himself thinking about Struther Cady and a cache of twenty grand.

He sat staring thoughtfully at Dreamer's Mountain for a long time before riding down out of the trees and trailing Cady back to San Rafael.

Supper was a mostly silent affair, hardly surprising, all things considered. Although still anything but welcome on Tadpole land, Santone had been invited to spend that day at the spread by Caroline rather than have him and Trina go off someplace else, as the girl had threatened to do.

Throughout the meal, as he had been during the day, Santone was the essence of good manners and courtesy, used the correct cutlery, showed he knew how to handle servants, was obviously familiar with fine food and wines. And although the atmosphere was slightly strained there was no hint of conflict or contention until Caroline declined an invitation to join the couple in the parlour, instead claiming a headache and announced her intention of retiring early.

Then she dropped the bombshell.

She could not stop the couple either seeing one another or eventually marrying, she stated calmly enough. However, she still strongly disapproved of the relationship, a point on which she agreed whole-heartedly with her husband. And while on the subject of her husband . . .

'Mr Tillerman informed me that he warned you that should you marry our daughter, Mr Santone, Trina would be disinherited. While I alone have the decision I'm in accord with this one hundred per cent.'

She held up her hand to form a circle with fore-finger and thumb.

'Not one thin dime. I'm sorry, honey, but that is how it has to be. Of course I'm hoping this news might dampen Mr Santone's ardour. But if it doesn't, it might not be so terrible as you might think. Your father and I started with nothing, and look what we have now. The whole world, except for each other. . . .'

Caroline turned quickly and hurried from the room. Trina glanced at Santone, who seemed to have gone pale. Then he smiled quickly.

'She doesn't mean it, Trina. Everyone's stirred up today, thanks to Sam.'

'I'm afraid you're wrong, Emile. Mother means every word. I can tell. She can be as stubborn as a Missouri mule.' She linked her arm through his and rested her head on his chest. 'But money or inheritances aren't important to us, are they, darling? You said so yourself.'

'Of course not.' So he said. But the expression on his face as he stared out over Trina's shoulder at the moonwashed acres of the Tadpole beyond the huge windows said something entirely different.

The 3.15 to Pima City clanked into the depot at the end of the fifty-mile run from Carbonne that rainy afternoon several days later, and a mackinawed and big-hatted Sam Tillerman was the first passenger to alight. He was greeted, not by family, friends or even a pretty woman but rather by a squat gentleman in fine threads sheltering beneath an enormous black umbrella clutched in the hand of a skinny assistant.

The tycoon had any number of assistants on hand today as befitted a man who built real railroads the way other men built models. The boss of the Colorado Line wanted to impress Tillerman, yet discovered he was wasting his time even before they'd reached the shelter of the waiting-room.

Tillerman was not here to to be impressed, intimi-dated, socialized or otherwise influenced by what-ever plans the tycoon might have had in mind for him.

Tillerman was here representing the Verdant Valley Association, currently engaged in vital discus-sion with both the Colorado Line and the Indian West Railroad Company to the north.

'Obsessive!' his ex-wife had snorted when informed of his involvement in this squabble which had absolutely nothing to do with him.

Of course, had she sat down to think about it calmly and rationally she would have realized it was nothing obsessional, merely characteristic.

Tillerman couldn't take it easy, not for a month, a week or a day. He had to be constantly active and with the Santone business dragging its heels, and him buzzing around the town, it wasn't long before the Association had sensed an opportunity and put him on the payroll.

He had two or three other irons in the fire as well, had to admit he was enjoying wheeling, dealing, cutting down tall poppies on behalf of people who'd once been close friends here.

The Colorado Line's big boss craved the valley's business, as it was one of the highest producers of cattle, grain and wool in that section of the Territory. Trouble was, his line's rates were way too steep, a fact of which Tillerman had reminded him before getting to light up his first cigar.

'Fairest rates in the West, Mr Tillerman. And cut to

the bone. Can't come down one cent.'

'Then we've got nothing to talk about.'

The tycoon paled. There was an air of finality in the tone of Tillerman who had only recently taken on the Verdant Valley assignment for a hefty fee, and was anxious to wrap it up this rain-sodden Thursday in order to get back to Greeley by Saturday.

'You can't be serious, man,' said the tycoon. 'And what are your qualifications anyway, might I ask? Are you sure you understand the railroad business?'

'The railroads are at the end of the Great Boom,' declared Tillerman, lighting up. 'Six months ago, passenger rates on the Colorado Line and the Indian West from Missouri to California via Colorado were around a hundred and twenty dollars. Back then, settlers were still pouring West, and land speculation here was going wild. Towns were staked out any old places, land prices soared and just about everything and anything that had once gone by wagon was now running on steel rails. Men like you were making profits like you had your own mints to make money.' He gusted a cloud of smoke. 'Right?'

'Well, er . . . yes, I suppose, if you want to put it that way—'

'Past tense,' Tillerman rapped, poking the man's pudgy chest. 'You both started cutting rates six months back, and now that hundred and twenty dollar ticket can be bought for ninety dollars, even less. But freight rates have stayed high, telling people like me that you and Indian West are in collusion. Well, that doesn't suit me, so it does not suit the Valley. I'm here to offer you the chance to get the jump on your competitor by bringing down your freight rates thirty per cent. Do that and you'll get Verdant Valley's business. Turn me down and I'll go to Indian West and offer them our trade for just ten per cent off.'

'Thirty per cent? That's impossible! Outrageous!'

'Is that yes or no?'

The tycoon was flustered as he glanced at his associates.

'Damnation! I'll need time to consider this—'

'Time to contact Indian West and hatch another fall-back price together, you mean? Sorry, no extensions of time. I'm booked on a train to take me to Greeley tonight.' Tillerman fished a green-covered folder from beneath his mackinaw.

'I've got a new contract listing the charges at my new prices here. Sign now and you've got one hell of a deal, stall and you'd better buy stock in Indian West. It's your call.'

After a further half-hour's haggling with an unshakeable Tillerman – rain pounding down on the tin roof – the tycoon sent an assistant off for a double brandy, drank it down, accused Tillerman of being illegitimate, a bandit and a disgrace to Colorado, then put his John Henry on the contract and it was done.

This was the largest commission Tillerman had earned in years, yet for some reason he was glum and brooding on the night train to Greeley. He was often that way these days. He was hoping Marie Elena might help lighten things up for him. That was if she didn't shoot him. Unpredictable, those redheads with a generous dash of Spanish blood. But then he was never quite sure which way dark-haired Irish beauties might jump either. Maybe it was him? Perish the thought!

Struther Cady came awake with the first light coming up behind Dreamer's Mountain. He sat up stiffly, stretching his arms and grunting a little. The years in jail might have toughened him both physically and mentally, yet the long saddle hours and hard physical work he'd been putting himself through out here, fifty miles north-east of San Rafael, over the past several days, was wearing him out some.

Tentatively he flexed the left knee he'd fallen upon and scraped during a high-climbing exercise on a rock face just on dusk last night. The joint clicked but the stiffness was less noticeable than it had been overnight. Maybe sleeping under the stars on grass beneath a Fort Union blanket was not as good for you as some outdoorsmen claimed.

He shucked the blanket aside and drew on his boots, then massaged warmth and colour into his face with those calloused rockyard hands.

Instinctively he buckled on his gun belt. He removed the .45 and spun the cylinder as he surveyed his surroundings. Nothing stirring but some kingbirds in a thicket. On and off yesterday while he'd been scouring arroyos, fissures, side canyons and gully-washes – in between clambering over boulders and shinning around cliffs – he'd had a feeling he'd not experienced since his days on the owlhoot with Lucas McCoy: a feeling that someone was watching him. Of course it was a free country. A man could watch whatever or whomever he liked, within reason. Still, it was not a feeling he enjoyed, and it relaxed him some to realize there was as yet no sign of it's returning this morning.

He rose, stretched and massaged his stubbled jaw.

This was a markedly different man from the ex-con who'd ridden into San Rafael weeks earlier. Then he had been taut and eager with a sense of urgency about him, wary of a hostile reception, eager to be accepted at least to the point where he could concentrate on what had brought him here and not have to worry about some citizen with a grudge and a long memory maybe trying to square accounts for something that had happened a decade ago with a .44.

This early-rising Struther Cady appeared shabbier and less sure of himself, despite the fact that he came and went in San Rafael these days without anyone paying him much mind one way or the other. In reality he looked exactly like a man who had been hungrily reaching out for something big, clawing for the brass ring of triumph and riches, only to wind up with two handfuls of nothing and thinning prospects.

And such was the case.

Naturally Cady had headed to San Rafael post haste upon his release from Duell Basin to take up the search for the $20,000 missing ever since the hold-up. He'd had these plans, carefully mulled over and refined over countless jailhouse nights, whereby he expected to get to solve the big mystery of the Westland Bank haul in a hurry. These notions, however, had largely depended on a certain key player in that long-ago drama of theft, pursuit and violent death, namely Big Sam Tillerman, late of Tadpole Ranch. It was upon this rock that the Cady high hopes had foundered.

It had been pure luck that saw a rare Tillerman visit home coincide with Cady's arrival in San Rafael. But that was about as lucky as it got. His attempts to ingratiate himself with Tillerman had been curtly brushed aside even before the big man got himself involved in a domestic conflict, resulting in his now having forked his bronc and vanished, leaving Cady with optimism and ideas and precious little hope of realizing them.

He'd expected all along that securing Tillerman's assistance in his treasure-hunt would prove anything but easy. But it had been a dream that kept him sane and alive.

Tillerman was the only man living who could possibly have some idea – no matter how vague – of exactly where the bank money lay.

Cady had to believe that if he believed nothing else.

He had known McCoy well and was now getting to know Tillerman. McCoy would have hung on to the money and kept riding while ever he could stay in the saddle; he was that breed. Wounded badly enough to succumb eventually, he'd reached Dreamer's with Tillerman on his hammer. He'd been hounded until forced in the end to climb down and conceal the swag. His next step – had he been strong enough – would have been to lead his pursuer as far from the stash as possible before making his last stand – and even Tillerman had subsequently admitted it had been a gutsy one.

So where had McCoy got down?

Only Tillerman knew and he had never told a single greedy treasure-hunter one damn thing; he knew that for a fact. Whether McCoy had stashed the loot where he'd dismounted, or whether he'd managed to stagger a further mile or ten through the deep snowdrifts, Tillerman was the one and only who could indicate the exact locality where the last act of the drama had taken place.

Cady massaged his unshaven jaw slowly, pensively. The gods must hate him. Where would you find a less approachable hard-nosed son of a bitch than that high-stepper! Blood from a stone would surely be easier.

But he couldn't quit. Not now.

Without Tillerman's assistance he had been reduced to doing what hundreds, perhaps thousands of hopefuls had done before him in seaching for the Big Twenty.

Yet there was one vital distinction between Struther Cady and every wide-eyed hopeful who had engaged in the great treasure hunt. Every man Jack of them, from Sheriff Poole down to the busboy from the Paramount Hotel, had confined their search to the Marble Canyon sector of Dreamer's Mountain where McCoy's and Tillerman's hoofprints had vanished in the snow. Only Cady knew of the significance of the upper Marble Canyon region, and he would comb it until he dropped.

He quit the canyon and climbed towards his hidden campsite.

The outlaw had shown his mettle a thousand times in the big house. He was showing it now. Guts and an iron will had kept him live throughout his ten-year nightmare. The same qualities might well carry him to his grave unless he either got miraculously lucky out here in the wilds, or else somehow managed to parley with Tillerman again.

From his lofty campsite, he stared out over this lopsided valley, lying green and beautiful under a warm morning sun following the rain.

He was trying to picture this terrain blanketed in white with knifing winds cutting through the trees on a day so bitter-cold that even the winter critters had holed up, leaving their territory to two hard men with guns.

He checked out his horse and pack-mule before releasing them to wander down to the rich grass while he fixed himself some chow.

The camp-fire was soon crackling on fresh, dry fuel. As the Arbuckle's boiled, Cady hunkered on his spurs with a can of peaches and a Bowie knife in his hands. Fruit breakfast for a tough man? It still beat Duell Basin fodder hands down. His rifle leaned within reach close by as he sipped coffee and ate, his eyes never still. With the knife, he speared each half-peach, sliced it in half and lifted the piece into his jaws with the tip of the knife. He kept the knife well-honed and the blade reflected sunlight as he ate. Then he glimpsed the image of head and shoulders in the bright steel and realized he was no longer alone.

Cady's reaction was instinctive, his actions as supple and explosive as those of a big cat disturbed at its feeding.

He snatched up the Winchester and was rolling with it in his hands when the man in the rocks behind called to him:

'Don't get excited, Cady. We're all pards here, aren't we?'

Cady was on his back, rifle extended, finger on the trigger and ready to cut loose. Slowly the blued barrel came down as the intruder stepped into the open. Cady was at once both pleased and alarmed to recognize his sometime drinking partner from town, Emile Santone.

CHAPTER 6

ROUGH COMPANY

By the time daylight came to Tadpole Ranch Caroline had been abroad two hours. That the work of the mistress of any 15,000-acre cattle kingdom was never done was a fact she freely acknowledged and accepted. Yet it was not simply accounts, pasture management, freight costs, Army contracts or even her daughter's ongoing liaison with an undesirable suitor that were responsible for her rising so much earlier and sleeping less well.

These life habits had in fact become her regular pattern from the very day she'd stood on the upper front balcony of the ranch house with the morning sun warm upon her face, watching the tall-in-the-saddle figure of her ex-husband disappear along the town trail up Idiot Ridge.

And every night she put away a half-bottle of blended bourbon, another habit she felt she could well do without.

A routine of hard liquor, late nights and too-early

mornings might take the glow from most women's cheeks but as yet seemed to have no such effect upon Caroline Tillerman.

She attributed this to a strong constitution, along with the fact that she sprang from a long line of rugged County Kildare boozehounds who could laugh, carouse, dance and in general raise hell with the very best and never show much the worse for it unless called upon to mix their pleasure with something as mundane and debilitating as honest work.

Thus far, she was discovering she could do both. What bothered her every day was why her life patterns should have altered so dramatically in recent years – although it was possible she knew the reason all too well and simply did not want to acknowledge it.

Drinking or dry, happy or sad, one thing still gave her the same pleasure as always. That was simply strolling through the fine house she'd helped design and build. She preferred doing this when everything was still and quiet. Early morning or late at night were her favourite times.

She now stood just inside the entrance of what they called the 'South Room'. This was her favourite section of the house despite the fact that it was a very masculine room which smelled richly of leather and wax. No frills or feminine furbelows here. Just solid, heavy, dark furnishings, brass fittings, brooding landscapes on the walls. There was a pipe-rack, liquor cabinet, a surprisingly comprehensive and well-used library of leather-bound books. Above the hearth mantle hung a portrait of a tall and striking couple in wedding-day finery.

It was too early in the day for melancholy, Caroline told herself. Besides, she didn't really feel that way this morning despite all the reasons she might have had for doing so. There were days when a body felt upbeat and positive even if the wells were low, the prime bull had busted out of its enclosure and your first cup of morning coffee tasted like swill.

Today was such a day for the mistress of Tadpole, and she found she could gaze up at that photographic portrait of Samuel and Caroline Tillerman without regret, only remembering the good times of which there surely had been many. Selectively she recalled a June morning following a black night when rustlers struck the west graze and Sam had led the full crew off in pursuit. Throughout much of the night, the distant stutter of gunfire rolled across the long-grass plains, and before first light Caroline was out on the range in the buckboard, not knowing whether she had been widowed overnight.

Then the rising sun exploded over Red Cow Hill and with it came her husband, seemingly larger than life, astride a huge bay horse, alone, having left the men to mop up what was left of the cow-thieves, impelled to come racing back across the slopes for the headquarters – by what? Intuition that she would be there? Or might that not have been actual certainty? She remembered his arms going about her and hugging her for an eternity . . . back in those early days of high spirits and true love. Before the ogres of friction, recrimination, abrasive personalities and mutually aggressive natures came to share this grand hacienda with them.

And very importantly and tellingly now, or so it seemed, before Sam got to do so much negotiating, wheeling-dealing, hatching deals and mingling with the power élite, and so much less hands-on stuff like bronco-busting, trail-driving and punching it out with lazy cowhands or crooked dealers.

She sighed.

She'd always wanted him to be successful. When he got there she wanted him sweaty, cussing and unshaven again. How did you figure?

She crossed to the huge windows which faced the south. Standing there for some time, she watched the mists clear from the Fritz River bottomlands and the day's first eagle take to the skies far out above Dreamer's Mountain.

And wondered where he was at that moment. Winding up an all-night cards-and-whiskey session with high-roller wheeler-dealers of his own ilk, perhaps. Or maybe he was on a train hammering across the endless prairies, boots on the seat opposite, chewing a cigar and jotting down figures on a notepad, figuring how to rake off the top percentage from the next deal for Samuel T. Tillerman. And not a thought for his ex-wife and the burden of her ever-increasing concerns over their daughter in all probability.

That last thought crept in under her cheerful guard somehow, and Caroline banished it instantly. Not today, she promised herself. She was determined to remain cool, calm and positive on this bright Thursday despite the fact this was scheduled to be the day she had agreed to sit down with Trina and finalize plans for the wedding.

She was, of course, prepared to spare nothing to give her one-and-only the finest wedding Turlock County had ever seen, despite the fact that in a way she would prefer seeing Trina throw herself away on a stable-hand.

There had been several blazing rows over the past fortnight since the family attorney finished drawing up the necessary documents which would see Trina disinherited from the moment she said 'I do'.

Caroline had been implacable in this regard, unshakeable. One of the few things she and Tillerman had agreed upon totally during his last chaotic visit was their belief that Emile Santone was patently a fortune-hunter looking to get his claws into the Tillerman wealth. Family friend Sheriff Poole shared that opinion. It had been hard for Caroline to maintain her rigid position on this, especially when she had to do so alone without Trina's father to support her. But she was accustomed to such situations; she wondered if Sam would even bother turning up for the wedding in light of his antipathy towards the prospective groom and that three-way fight which had rocked the South Room to its foundations.

Caroline half-smiled as she turned to make her way across gleaming, polished floorboards.

At least they still fought with the old passion, she reflected. That was one thing that had not been diluted or corroded by separation.

Sam always appeared surprised by her feistiness in battle; she in turn was uncomprehending when he didn't cave in to her the way she could cause most other men to do whenever she chose.

She halted abruptly. Her daughter stood in the hall doorway staring at her. Trina was red-eyed, and a dark bruise showed on the side of her pretty chin. She looked terrible, yet there was a strange air of calm resignation about her which her mother recognized as she ran to her and took her hands.

'Honey, what's wrong? What happened to your face?'

'It's over, mother.'

'What?'

The girl broke away and moved to the impressive fieldstone fireplace, above which hung a pair of crossed sabres and the colours of the regiment her father had fought with during the War Between the States.

'We had a terrible row,' Trina said quietly. A pause, then: 'I suppose you can guess what it was about?'

'The inheritance?'

Trina nodded her dark head, not meeting her gaze now.

'You were right, Mother, you and Father. About Emile, I mean. He was drinking last night and it all came out. He . . . he wanted me to engage an attorney and sue for what he calls my legal rights. He said terrible things about you and Father. He was like a stranger. And when I tried to reason with him, he struck me. That was when I returned his ring and told him I never wanted to see him again.'

Although Caroline's heart ached to see her daughter's pain, at the same time it sang. She felt all her prayers were answered as she drew the girl's head to

99

her breast and encouraged her to cry it all out.

She looked up at the portrait. In that light and at this angle, Sam appeared to be smiling.

Marie Elena slept late that morning. With good reason. Their brawling, boozing reunion had consumed eighteen high-emotion hours and she was all played out. Even so, she awakened in the huge four-poster feeling totally marvellous, stretched languorously and purred like a big glossy cat as she brushed a banner of red hair from her eyes and reached out for him.

She jolted upright.

She was all alone. Again!

'Tillerman!'

No response. Bare feet hit the floor and mid-morning Sneak Creek was treated to the spectacle of its most statuesque and flimsily clad beauty appearing on the first-floor balcony of the skinny-ribbed hotel with a bottle in one hand and what appeared to be a gun in the other.

It was a gun.

Deep in their cups overnight as the jewelled stars followed their eternal courses across the heavens, the couple had vowed eternal fealty even though neither seemed quite to comprehend the meaning of the words. Love forever. Never to part. Eternal bliss. All this and more. Yet here in the sober light of morning, with the day hardly begun, he had already left her.

'Tillerman, you bastard!'

Her imperious cry attracted the attention of the

street-sweeper, the general storekeeper, a locksmith *en route* to a job, a trio of ragged wolf-hunters purchasing ammunition across the street at the gunsmith's, the hotelkeeper, two affronted matrons and the driver of the rusted red water-cart creaking by. But no response from Big Sam Tillerman.

And yet Marie Elena's lover heard that shout quite clearly as he calmly curried his Appaloosa in the hotel stables and viewed the new morning through an expensive Cuban cigarillo smoke haze.

His saddle stood close by, soaped, cleaned, dried, polished and ready to be flung across the animal's sturdy back at a moment's notice.

That sudden cursing cry was his moment's notice.

He threw on the saddle and was tightening the cinch when the gunshot sounded, rumbling down one-horse Sneak Creek's main stem like a cannon blast. Sounded like the lady was really getting sore.

Tillerman fitted boot to stirrup but did not swing up. It was not like him to be indecisive. He could have been gone in one swift drumbeat of hoofs, but instead he slowly lowered his boot to terra firma, handed the reins to a wide-eyed stable-boy and started across the sunwashed yard.

Who was he trying to kid? There were big empty spaces in his life when he was alone, yet as soon as he got halfway close to someone, all he could think of was hightailing. Marie Elena might be bad-tempered, flighty, oversexed, more than just a little violent at times and was constantly threatening to run off and marry a millionaire copper-king suitor she had stashed away someplace in Arizona. But in her own

101

way she understood him, which took some doing.

The eye-catching figure up on the balcony was getting ready to shoot again when he appeared below. She pointed the gun at him, then spun the weapon on her finger and scowled.

'Where were you going?'

He shrugged. 'No place in particular.'

'You're dressed for the trail. And your saddle-bags are missing from the room. Our room.'

'So?'

'So, were you by any chance thinking of running back to your wife?'

Tillerman's face darkened. This scene lacked dignity. He should be offended and maybe he was. But she still had great legs.

Before he could reply, Marie Elena leaned on the balcony railing and said:

'You've been acting strange ever since you came back from the South, mister. All moody and quiet, you are. If I didn't know better I'd think you were still in love with your wife.'

'Ex-wife. And do you have to tell the whole damn town?'

'Why don't you get back up here where you belong and I won't have to shout, pilgrim.'

Sneak Creek, some nine-tenths of which now formed a wide-eyed audience for this real-life drama, watched Tillerman massage his jaw, get rid of his Cuban, mutter to himself, then make for the stairs. Even so he appeared almost reluctant as he climbed. Shifting their gaze from him to the stirring figure waiting for him on the balcony every man, greybeard and beardless boy, thought there must be something wrong with him if he felt the way he looked.

Maybe they were right.

Emile Santone steered his horse towards the hitch rack of Kelly Street's finest saloon with Struther Cady following him in. By this time Cady's ongoing presence in town scarcely raised a ripple of interest, while his new pard remained popular and accepted just about any place he chose to visit within the San Rafael city limits.

The riders contrasted sharply as they swung from their saddles, the ex-inmate of Duell Basin lean, hard-muscled and close-cropped in prison-issue rig, Santone eye-catching and impressive with that head of golden curls and the trim, athletic body of a wrestler enhanced by smart and expensive tailoring. Although the pair might be seen sinking a cold one together occasionally or sitting in on the same game at the Ten-Bar or the Slake My Dry, they'd not been sighted openly riding together until today by the lazy porch-rocker observers of life who were watching this Coloradan summer drowse by.

There was good reason for this. Santone and Cady had not been any place outside town until today. The two had met way out at Dreamer's Mountain, and Struther Cady was still to learn just how and why this had come about.

During the long ride back to town, Santone had been uncommunicatively sober and almost sombre, in sharp contrast with his familiar geniality and smiling good humour.

Cady got the impression that this dangerous man from the South had plenty on his mind today, but was not given any reason for this until they'd crossed the Ten-Bar porch where they removed their hats and stood swabbing away sweat before going in to order.

They took their bottle to a corner table out of earshot of the losers propping up the long bar.

Santone still appeared tight around the jawline but at least seemed ready to talk again. His brooding silences could make even tough Cady uneasy at times.

'You know something? A man can travel a long way in twenty-four hours without going anywhere, Cady.'

Cady's brow rutted in puzzlement. This sounded deep. Deep thought was not one of his characteristics. Whenever folks got all mysterious and meaningful on him he tended to lose interest.

'Huh,' he grunted.

'Yessir, a man surely can,' Santone insisted. He took a swig and topped up his glass from the bottle, hooked a thumb behind a flashy belt buckle. 'This time yesterday I was staring big money square in the eye. I was seeing me in a house big as this saloon, more cattle than a man could count in a week, a cellarful of the finest booze in the country, good-looking women, fine carriages and senators and tycoons stopping off for supper Saturday nights and calling me buddy. Today? If I don't get lucky at the tables tonight I just might have to shift into one of those clapboard flop-houses along Silleck Street. Tillerman's busted up me and his girl and she does-n't want to see me any more – the uppity bitch. Sugar to shit, Cady. Life can be like that, you'd better believe.'

Cady was silent for a spell.

He liked this man despite the fact that he felt he didn't really know him. People hinted Santone had a past, whatever that was supposed to mean. Cady had a past. A real one. And thus far he hadn't heard about Santone shooting up towns or having a judge with a port-wine complexion and hatred in his eyes sentence him to ten years hard – as had been his fate.

But that Santone knew his way around the twilight world of gamblers, percentage girls, hustlers, con men, rogues and rustlers as he did himself, there was no doubt. He didn't know enough about the man yet to rate him a fellow rider of the owlhoot. However, he did assess him as a man with a ruthless streak and mighty high on ambition who regularly hinted at big prospects.

Was Santone now hinting that those prospects didn't exist for him any more? He was careful how he put this thought into words when he responded. But Santone did not take offence, just sighed, folded his arms and nodded.

'Got it in one, Cady. The big wedding's off. *Finito, adios muchacho.* Two months' hard work down the chute – just like that.'

'I don't get it. Are you saying romancing that fine-looking girl was work?'

'*Amigo,* nothing's harder work than pretending you're in love with someone when you ain't. All that sweet-talking, lying, behaving yourself and trying to get along with her folks and stuff. You reckon busting

105

rocks in the big house is tough? Vacation time compared to trying to sweet talk your way into a fortune – you can believe that.'

Cady sipped his liquor as he considered. Somehow the loser role didn't seem to fit Santone, he mused. He'd had the impression he and that girl were about as tight as a couple could get, despite the family opposition.

The Santone-Trina Tillerman romance had been the prime topic of conversation around San Rafael until temporarily relegated to second place by Cady's return.

But following Sam Tillerman's visit, highlighted by bloody fist-fights and domestic upheaval out at Tadpole Ranch, the courtship, the planned nuptials and the Tillermans' threat to disinherit their daughter had seen the whole matter re-established as the number one topic of interest, a position it had held ever since.

Cady figured that just about every bank bandit, hold-up artist, con man, twister, crook and snake-oil salesman in the West dreamed of marrying rich and leaving the shady side of the trail for ever. But achieving this dream took a special kind of talent which, he reckoned, Emile Santone had in spades. Now Santone was talking like a loser and Cady's curiosity was piqued.

'Mum and Dad won out in the end, is all,' Santone continued, as though reading his thoughts. The man's familiar flinty-eyed look was back as through the open window he watched the stage for Sky Cloud Lake draw away from the depot, teamers champing at the bit and eager to run. His lips compressed. 'Big man, Tillerman!' His voice was thick with venom now. 'But of course, like they say, bigger they are the harder they fall. I'm wondering now if I shouldn't have taken the bull by the horns right at the outset and given that big prick six in the guts. It's real amazing how small a big man looks lying at your feet with his lights and liver splattered all over the street.'

The brutal words and the way they were spoken aroused a curious excitement within Struther Cady, a feeling almost of brotherhood. It was crystal-clear to him now. Behind his façade, Santone was stamped from the same metal as himself. Iron.

He began to shape a cigarette. It was quiet in the big room. A moth bumbled about a lamp near the window.

Cady's thoughts ran deep.

Lucas McCoy was the last honest-to-God pard he'd had. He'd never felt the need of another in the ten years since. Yet raking Santone up and down with shrewd, deep-set eyes he found himself suddenly wondering if it might not be time to change that situation.

Cady lighted the quirly from the top of the lamp cylinder. He watched the smoke lift and waver in the updraft and then drift through the open window. Santone was studying him with an intense expression as though anticipating response to his big statement.

Yet Cady would not be hurried as he mentally ran the other through the Struther Cady Qualifications List.

On the credit side, Santone shaped up remarkably

well. He was smart, impressive, double tough, ambitious and a proven dab hand with guns and horses. He'd just taken a big fall and was plainly ripe for a deal – and Cady might have a deal in his hip pocket if only he could get to swing it. But there were questions about Santone, one or two in particular that would have to be answered before he would be making any overtures.

'Why'd you tag me this morning?' he said flatly.

'Simple. I figured you might lead me to the money.'

Santone was disarmingly straight; Cady decided it was time to plunge right in.

'Do I get the hunch you're talking about the hold-up money, Santone?'

'What else?'

'My partner cached it some place and not even I knew where.'

'Do you know "Johnny's in the Cold Ground"?'

'What?'

'That's another good song you could sing, Cady.'

'I'm telling you the truth.'

'Then how come I sat and watched you for two hours digging, climbing, scratching and nosing about the way you were doing twenty miles from Black Rocks this morning, desperado? What were you searching for as though your life depended on it if it wasn't the twenty thousand?'

Santone's menacing smile appeared again. There was something satanic about the hook of the eyebrows and the glimmer of the eyes as he studied Cady without blinking once.

'Come on, Struther, don't insult a man with that blank look. As soon as they told me the story of you and your partner and the big *dinero* – after you showed up ten years almost to the day – I figured you just had to be after the money. Nothing else made sense. So I've been keeping tabs on you ever since, in between all the moonlight and fiddle-music sessions with Trina. And what I saw today after I tagged you all the way out there told me loud and clear my hunch had to be one hundred per cent right.'

Before Cady could reply the figure attired in vest, flat-brimmed Stetson and star paused below them out on the plankwalk. As usual, Sheriff Poole managed to appear both relaxed and authoritative, the very picture of a man capable of controlling a sizeable town without raising either his voice or a fuss.

'Evening, gentlemen.'

The two nodded guardedly. Both were circumspect where Nate Poole was concerned. He knew a great deal about Santone and most everything about Cady. Not much point in either trying to convince this man that they were anything than what they really were.

'Pretty night, Sheriff.' Santone smiled. 'If I felt any better I might shoot myself.'

No answering smile from the lawman.

'I spoke with Mrs Tillerman today, mister,' he said. 'I didn't much care for what I heard.'

'Why, what might that be, Sheriff?'

'I rarely place much stock in hearsay, but with a woman like Caroline Tillerman she could tell me the sky was falling and I would believe her. So let me tell you something plain, Santone. If you threaten Miss Trina or her mother again I'll have you on your way to Duell Basin in chains so fast you won't feel your feet leave the ground. Do I make myself clear?'

Santone just nodded. He looked relaxed but was far from it. He was holding it all in, sitting on his suppressed explosiveness. The falling-out with Trina Tillerman had exposed great cracks in his smooth façade. Cady sensed the man wanted to take the badgeman apart right then and there, had to admire the way he kept it all bottled up and throttled back. Another plus point for Emile Santone.

'And you are still here, Cady, I see,' Poole went on, switching the point of his attack. Plainly the spectacle of two men of questionable character hobnobbing openly was not to Poole's liking. 'With no good reason that I can see.'

Cady didn't know what to say so said nothing. This appeared to be the right tactic when Poole just fingered his moustache and moved off along his street at his own steady pace.

'Him too,' Santone said softly.

'Him too, what?'

'Six in the guts.'

The remark was delivered with such force that it stripped away whatever last reservations Cady might have been harbouring towards Trina Tillerman's ex. He was now convinced that behind his urbane veneer, Santone was a blood-brother – and Struther Cady's blood ran darkly.

Until today Cady had believed that the only one who could help him recover the Westland fortune

110

was the man who had hounded McCoy all the way to Dreamer's Mountain that day. Tillerman.

Yet despite the plans he'd hashed and rehashed in prison, Cady had always feared it would prove to be somewhere between tough and impossible to get anywhere close to Tillerman, much less get the man involved in his recovery search.

So it had proved.

Tillerman had shown that no amount of sweet syrup or bogus admiration coming from any jailbird bank robber could possibly impress him. So he'd figured he'd have to go it alone, until today's events jolted him back to reality.

He needed someone. It was too big a job to handle alone.

Sure, it could be high risk inviting an outsider in on a deal that had been exclusively his ever since McCoy's body had been brought back to San Rafael across his horse by Tillerman. But when had he ever been too yellow to take a risk?

He worked up saliva in his mouth and swallowed it. The back of his shirt was sticking to him. He could feel nervous sweat trickling down his sides as Santone turned his face towards him and arched an eyebrow.

'That's some look you are giving me, jailbird. You worried about what I said about the tinstar?'

Cady blurted it out. 'How would you like to make an easy ten thousand bucks, Santone?'

Santone reacted like a man who had been waiting to hear those exact words all his shady life.

CHAPTER 7

KIDNAPPED!

Everyone in Carbonne knew Sam Tillerman from earlier visits and nobody wanted to tangle with him. They admired his energy and success but were also very much aware he was a hard and often difficult man. He threw himself into everything he undertook with drive and purpose, and whatever he wanted done had better be done properly and on schedule, otherwise the fur would surely fly.

As a consequence when Tillerman's familiar figure appeared at the head of the street that morning just after opening time at the saloon, the bartender was wary.

There was a rumour going round that Big Sam's visit to their mayor and land agent in his role as representative of a bunch of nesters camped out along Creche Creek had not gone well. Seemed the mayor was insisting the nesters move on to facilitate the sale of the Creche Creek strip in toto to a big combine from across the border, while Tillerman had insisted even more loudly that the mayor was a thief, rogue and son of a bitch with no knowledge of or respect for the Homestead Act.

Sounded like the recipe for big trouble to the bartender, who found an excuse to scuttle out back as bootheels thudded on his porch. This left the bar in the temporary care of a big-busted blonde who, because she never betrayed one trace of fear for the wild men with bushy beards who came howling in from the oil rig on Dust Desert once a month looking to get their rocks off, was unlikely to be too fazed by just one big man with a short fuse clutching a piece of paper in his fist.

And smiling.

That grin caused the blonde to blink uncertainly as Tillerman sauntered across to the bar and dropped her a big genial wink, for this was no easy-smiling man.

'A cold beer, sweetheart, and whatever you are having.'

There was a clatter in back. The bartender who had been crouched by a chink in the wall, watching, had lost his balance in surprise.

'And a double for Wiley,' Tillerman insisted loudly. 'Good barkeep, that Wiley. And you're a good woman too. I can tell by the way you draw a beer.'

The woman grew even more uneasy. Tillerman was rarely genial, much less affable. Was this some kind of plot to lull the place into a state of false security before the big man exploded?

This seemed a reasonable suspicion. Yet well before customer, girl and bartender had finished their drinks, Wiley and the blonde realized their unease was unfounded. Tillerman showed them his document. It was a Letter of Intent drawn up by an attorney and signed by the mayor-cum-land agent, attesting that he no longer intended trying to evict the nesters from Creche Creek either now or in the future.

'How,' Wiley had to ask, 'did you do it?'

The Tillerman smile was smug as he folded the document and slipped it into his hip pocket.

'Someone checked out the mayor's herds at the mesa yesterday,' he informed. 'He found a dozen or more cows with blotched brands. Badly blotched, they were at that. The original brands were still readable. Crossed Ts. The marshal of Donninger has been hunting for that stolen stock for weeks, so. . . .'

He didn't finish. Didn't have to. This was plainly a typical Tillerman coup. He'd nailed the mayor for rustling, but instead of turning him in had blackmailed him into quitting his campaign against the nesters. The big man had done this sort of thing before, but in this case the difference was that his good humor was still as evident when he left as it had been on his arrival. Which posed the question: was it remotely possible Sam Tillerman could be mellowing?

The answer to this was a resounding no. But despite a testy disposition aggravated by recent unsettling experiences back in Turlock County, Tillerman often enjoyed a period when things seemed to go right, successes tumbled into his lap and he found himself able to avoid situations which resulted in angry words or even fist-fights in public places.

The good mood was still riding with him when he crossed the county line and entered the Sky Cloud Lake region later the same day. There was the first hint of autumn in the air. Soon the leaves would be turning, but today everything was green, gold and blue. Red was waiting for him at the lake town of Rand Water, and Sam Tillerman felt curiously at peace.

Not happy, of course. He had not been what you could rightly call happy since the day the divorce was finalized. But peace was a good substitute for happiness, he reflected, and providing Marie Elena didn't get to do or say anything to rile him tonight he saw no good reason why this easy mood should not continue.

Storm clouds were amassing across the placid waters of the lake when he raised the town, but the big horseman read no ominous portents in this. He had a good feeling that nothing could ruffle him tonight. Yet as destiny would have it, his uncharacteristically benign attitude was due to be challenged the very moment he strode into their Rand Water hotel room to find no sign of Red Sanchez or her belongings.

All that remained was the scrawled note on the bed which he snatched up with a muttered curse:

It read:

You're still crazy about your ex and you'll just dump me again as you did before, I know. So before you can do that, I'm dumping you. And don't even think of attending my wedding. Thanks for nothing, Romeo!

It was signed: *Soon to be Mrs Thaddeus Lorenzo Henry of Black Bluff – Mrs Sheriff Tad Henry to you, you two-faced rat.*

'Henry? That broken-winded jackass posing as a lawman?' Tillerman said feelingly. 'I thought he'd given up on her after the last three or four times I whisked her away from under his long red nose. . . .' He paused and shrugged. 'So who cares?' But he cared, less so because he realized this time she was gone for good than the simple fact that she had called the final shots, had enjoyed the last word. He liked to reserve that pleasure for himself.

He was about to screw up the note and hurl it from him, when he frowned. He scanned it again. What did that overheated redhead mean: *You will just dump me as you did before?*

He didn't have any plans for dumping anyone – especially not now. They had been scheduled to go sailing tomorrow and then . . .

He whirled at the sound of a discreet cough. He had left the door open. The desk clerk stood there nervously clutching two telegraph slips.

'Pardon me, Mr Tillerman, these are for you. I brought them up to you . . . er . . . to Miss Sanchez. But she threw them at me and began packing straight off. She seemed mighty upset, I'm afraid to say.'

Only then did Tillerman realize that the threatening storm had burst across Rand Water, the growling thunder and hammer of rain on the roof was apparently responsible for the weird sensation of sudden unease that prickled down his backbone. Or could there be another cause?

He snatched the slips from the man's hand and read them like someone having a bad dream. One wire was from Caroline telling him Trina had disappeared. The other, unsigned, informed him that his daughter had been abducted and that the writer would be contacting him in due course to instruct him on what he would be required to do if he wished ever to see her alive again.

The night was heavy with mystery and uncertainty.

There was a restless stirring in the canyons. A breath of sound coming down off the mesa might have been nothing more sinister than the wind, or could just as easily been a killer wolf slinking by as soft as a zephyr.

Even the snakes went still and wild animals were wary, their senses sifting sights, sounds and smells before they dared emerge from their lairs.

Or was this all just his overheated imagination at work?

Struther Cady, returning to the canyon from Hayes, rubbed a hand across his face where he sat his saddle motionless in the deep shadow of the butte.

He was too tough to fall prey to imagination, he chided himself. There was no good reason for the hunters to come this far north, or be hunting by night. Their search would be confined to San Rafael and its surrounds with the emphasis on the Monroe Road where Trina Tillerman's overturned buggy and unconscious escort had been found some thirty hours earlier.

There's nobody up here in the Old Country's canyons, ravines and mesas but you and the odd grey coyote, Cady. So wise up.

The self-lecture worked.

When he pushed the horse out of the shadow into the moonwash he was sitting straight in the saddle again, empty-handed and almost relaxed.

The stars were still, and in slanting moonlight the rocks cast their deepest shadows.

Hoofs clattered briskly against stone and gravel as he travelled on at the lope for Pico Canyon.

Once, in the company of Lucas McCoy, Cady had explored Pico Canyon at the remote northern limits of Turlock County as a possible emergency hideout following the bank job. They had not needed it. But it was the first bolt-hole that came to mind when he and Santone sat down together as full-fledged partners to draft the plan that could see them get either very rich or very dead. There were strange and deeply mysterious cliff dwellings in the canyon. Nobody seemed sure who had once dwelt here, where they had come from or where and why the Old Ones had eventually gone.

After some of the Navajo tribes had been relocated in northern New Mexico, most had drifted on further into the wide lands south of the Colorado and San Juan rivers. But none had ever ventured back into this bleak corner of the country where their ancestors had once dwelt.

This was an eerie, disturbing land and Indian

legend had it that the spirits of those ancient cliff-dwellers lingered still.

But practical Cady was armoured against nocturnal whisperings and distorting echoes as he followed the winding course of the canyon to raise eventually the towering landmark of Blue Park Butte. After rounding two stone corners further on, he slowed the horses to a walk as a stalwart figure with a rifle appeared on a slab of stone twenty feet above.

'Nice timing, pard,' Santone called down. 'All done?'

Cady nodded as he stiffly dismounted. It was a far piece from Pico Canyon to the telegraph station at Hayes.

'All done and no hitches,' he reported. 'By this I figure Big Sam's on his way home, snorting fire.'

'He can snort all he pleases,' Santone replied, reaching the canyon floor in a series of athletic bounds. 'You warned him in the wire not to breathe a word to anybody?'

'Sure thing.' Cady glanced upwards at the shadowed casements of ancient dwellings. 'She all right?'

'Fine and dandy.' Santone was charged with electric energy. For long weeks he had been restricted to playing the role of the ardent suitor and well-mannered gentleman about town in his coldly calculated campaign to marry rich. But now the shackles were off he was set free in a new situation far more fitting to his nature. Suddenly he was again living on the edge and boldly reaching out and grabbing for whatever he wanted. This felt much more like the real Emile Santone and nothing like a namby-pamby dude picking his way through the horse-apples on Kelly Street with a perfumed kerchief to his nostrils, minding his manners and playing the gent.

This was a real man's red-blooded scam.

The two clambered up to the ancient lodge together, where fragments of pottery, arrowheads and stone scrapers littered the floor.

Trina stood calmly by an aperture with arms folded, ignoring their arrival. She had not been harmed during the abduction. Santone, who had familiarized himself with her regular movements and habits prior to their final break-up, had simply intercepted her on her return from a visit to an aunt up in Greenville that night, had taken out her cowboy escort without effort, and it was all over. Convincing Cady that kidnapping – a sure-fire hanging offence in Colorado – was the only realistic way to bring Tillerman to them on his knees, had been much tougher. But once committed to the operation, Cady had shown his mettle.

'Good news, honey,' called Santone. 'The wire's gone to big daddy, so it shouldn't be long now before we get to do business. Then you'll be free as the wind.'

'You must be even stupider than I thought, Emile,' she snapped back. 'Father won't pay you a cent. He would rather die.'

Santone threw both hands theatrically wide. 'Who said a word about paying, Trina? All we'll be asking of Big Sam is that he guide us around the Marble Canyon region some. You know? Give us a hint where Cady's old dead pard planted twenty thousand under the snow. Can't see how a man would balk at that, especially when his daughter's life depends on it.'

'He'll kill you both. Ten of your kind wouldn't make half the man Father is.'

'See how a female can change her tune, Cady? A while back, Big Sam was the very worst in her eyes. Couldn't say enough bad about him and the way he treated her, she couldn't. Now? Why, suddenly Daddy's a hero ten feet tall and true blue. Amazing. OK, partner, we got some talking and planning to do.'

The pair climbed to a higher level where they could overlook the chamber and not be overheard. They were totally at ease in each other's company by this, bonded by success and the excitement that came with it.

'Well, the hard part's over already,' Santone congratulated himself as they sat smoking and drinking the good wine Cady had fetched back from Hayes.

'Tillerman's got no option but to play along if he wants to see Trina again.'

'Keeno.'

'What I still don't figure, is why, if he had got a good notion where the stash might be, Tillerman never made a bigger man of himself by hunting for it, or, if not that, why he never let anyone else in on his big secret.'

Cady looked wise.

'He was sick, shot-up and had a bellyful of that whole deal right then . . . leastwise that's how I see it. Already a handful of treasure-hunters had been beat up, shot up and killed as they hunted up there. So,

Tillerman didn't know exactly where it was and knew if he'd identified the general area he'd touch off a gold-rush and a whole lot of bloodshed.' Cady shrugged. 'So, being noble and civic-minded, the big fella figured it'd be best if he just kept his mouth shut and let the whole thing just blow away.'

'Uh huh. Makes a kind of sense, I guess.' Santone took a swig and winked. 'Only it didn't blow away, did it, *amigo*?'

'Not only didn't blow away. It's blown up right in that high-stepping sonuva's ugly pan! C'mon, drink up before I go pick up big daddy so we can lead him to the big *dinero* by the nose.'

They chinked their glasses and drank to San Francisco and the Barbary Coast where they planned to live like kings. And the ghosts of the Ancient Ones, murmuring and whispering in the night, troubled them not at all.

Big Sam was back!

The word spread through San Rafael like a brush fire fanned by a stiff westerly, and lawmen, possemen, citizens and even newsmen from out of town who'd arrived to cover the crime took fresh heart.

For this surely was a situation tailor-made for Tillerman, who was nothing if not at his best in a crisis.

Big Sam would know exactly what to do, who should do it and how. He was always that way when things went either right or wrong on a large scale. So, plainly all they had to do was sit back and take a breather while he assessed the full situation and began barking orders as only he could.

But all Tillerman did was to occupy a window table at the Ten Bar saloon with a shotglass and a bottle. From that vantage point he watched the restless comings and goings at the jailhouse across the street like a figure hewn from stone. Nobody could believe his Achilles heel had at last been pierced – that today saw him reduced to just another simple father rendered impotent by fear and grief.

Sheriff Nate Poole now felt obliged to ride in from the Lincoln Range search area after repeated requests for Tillerman to join him were ignored. 'What the devil is going on, Sam? Didn't you get my messages?'

Tillerman stared at the lawman like a stranger.

'She told me to get out of her life and stay out. That's what I'm doing.'

'Since when did you start doing anything anyone wants you to do?'

'Better get on with your work, Sheriff.' He poured another and slugged it down. 'Like I'm getting along with mine.'

Poole rarely lost his temper. He did so now. But it takes two to make a fight. Tillerman sat remote and detached, contributing nothing to the argument until the lawman flung from the barroom to spread the incredible news that Big Sam had finally cracked up right when he was most needed.

The old Tillerman would have raged, broken skulls, maybe even gone loco under such circumstances. Instead he just sat and drank whiskey that went down like water.

People came and went at the Ten Bar but none approached the solitary figure. None dared. That suited Sam, whose craggy, forbidding exterior effectively concealed what was going on inside. Everyone was of course talking kidnapping, but he was the only one who knew for certain. His little girl had been taken and he dare not breathe a word. Nate had posed the question – since when did he start doing what he was told? But this was different. He had no choice. Any scumsucker low enough to pull such a crime would surely not balk at murder if crossed or threatened.

Tillerman wouldn't push. Could not. Not even when everything in him screamed for action. He wanted to ride, search and spill blood. But he would not. He would sit here like a rock and allow San Rafael to pour its scorn upon him until the kidnappers contacted him.

If they did.

That was the horned worm of worry eating at his guts as he slugged his whiskey down. The county was crawling with searchers. What if they accidentally drew too close to the kidnappers? What if the scum lost their nerve? Might they not simply drag a blade across his daughter's slender neck and run?

Tillerman sat in pulsing silence, eyes closed, his heart clenched and painful in his chest. There was a beat like slow wings in his head as he came to understand what it was like to be a defender rather than an attacker. To be rendered one of the weak, no longer numbered amongst the strong.

Dusk was falling. The lamplighter made his

rounds. Tillerman was dimly conscious of the tempo of the saloon building up as the regulars drifted in to join haggard-eyed men taking a break from the search. He ignored it all, taking refuge in his detachment, the whiskey his only friend.

A sudden change in the barroom's tempo alerted him. He glanced up as the batwings swung inwards and his former ramrod came through. The man held the doors apart and Tillerman groaned inwardly when Caroline appeared, homing in on him like he was at Gettysburg again and she a Johnny Reb shell.

Nothing he could do but sit and take it. What in hell's name was wrong with him? she demanded. Why had he not come out to Tadpole? Was he ill? Didn't he understand what was happening? Tell her it wasn't spite over a foolish argument that was causing him to act this way. Tell her something. Anything.

But he'd received a terrible message warning him that one loose word would seal his daughter's fate.

'I'm drunk,' he slurred. 'I plan to stay this way. You should try it, honey . . .' A cold sweat gleamed along his jaw as he studied her broodingly from beneath heavy brows, and something wrenched inside him. 'Go home, Cal,' he said in a different voice. 'Just hold the fort out there, it's all you can do. But don't give up. Will you promise me that? Jory, take Mrs Tillerman home.'

Caroline's face was the colour of old pipeclay. She suddenly looked old, yet never more lovely. Tillerman yearned again for the old days, for the passion and fire . . . for the long rivers and green hills of Tadpole when it had been good. The three of them. His chest shuddered with convulsive breath and the hardness came to his face again.

'You still here, woman?'

He was thankful she left without another word, even though her parting look went through him like a knife. He shook his shoulders and stared down at his glass. He drank and drank again, until it was full night and he was on his feet and weaving for the doors, incapable of doing nothing any longer.

'Don't come back, Tillerman!'

'Big Sam, the big sham!'

They couldn't hurt him. They were fools to think they might.

The night air hit him hard and he was forced to lean against a lamp-post until his head stopped spinning. A hostile moon rocked in the sky. Falsefronts loomed menacingly and every face was an enemy's. He thrust away and moved on, willing himself to walk straight, enough pride left in him not to want to show weak before lesser men even though there was no strength in him.

He turned into an alley where none could see and allowed himself to stagger from side to side the way the whiskey insisted. Sober, he would have surely heard the steps behind, but drunk, they just sounded like his own echoes.

Then a voice:

'I wouldn't believe it if I didn't see it with my own eyes, Tillerman. You did just like we said.'

He turned sharply. The silhouette against the lighted backdrop of Kelly Street was wide in the shoulder and trim of hip, the voice familiar. He felt himself sobering as the figure stepped closer and he made out the cleft-chinned and dimpled smile of Emile Santone.

It hit him like a club to know he was looking at Trina's kidnapper.

CHAPTER 8

CANYON FURY

San Rafael's nearest town was Danziger, unpeeling
and raw, some fifteen miles to the north-west.
Danziger was but a few years old and comprised a
single main thoroughfare shaded by cottonwoods
and lined by unpainted falsefronted stores. This was
a one-doctor, two-saloon town, with water-troughs, a
deep well, a first-grade home-made whiskey and no
law office.

The journey had taken two hours and the saloon
was empty save for the man behind the bar when the
two dusty travellers showed around midnight.

The barman acted jittery but Tillerman thought
nothing of it. His attention was fixed on Santone as
the man paid for a flask and brought it and two
glasses to a centre table. Tillerman brushed the offer
of a drink aside with a curt gesture.

Their whole journey had been made in silence
with Santone refusing to be drawn out on anything.
If looks could kill, Trina's former suitor would be a

dead man. Maybe. Tillerman had to concede the uncertainty. He'd respected Santone as a hard man from their clashes, but knew now he'd vastly under-estimated him. This man, stripped of the façade he'd worn before, came across now like tempered steel. Totally dangerous.

'So . . . now we talk, Tillerman.' Santone straddled a chair with glass in hand, Tillerman's .45 was jutting now from his belt alongside his holstered Colt. The younger man appeared relaxed yet conveyed the impression of having a coiled spring in his body capa-ble of unleashing at a touch. 'What do you want to know?'

'Is my daughter alive?'

'Alive and well.'

'How much do you want?'

'Not a dime.'

'Don't play games with me, scum. How much?'

'Believe me, I'd like nothing better than to squeeze you for every last dime, Big Sam – you being the arro-gant piece of shit that you are. But I've seen those sorts of deals foul up before. There's too many things can go wrong in getting the *dinero* out of the bank, too many chances for a slick smartass like you to get messages out, pull a double-cross. Complications. So we forget trying to milk you dry. Anyway, this other deal is neat and clean, and, like I say, won't cost you a dime. Curious, aren't you?'

'Keep talking'

Santone obliged. And it was with a sense of shock that Tillerman began to realize that the kidnapping was only remotely linked with the break-up between

Trina and this man. That instead it had had its gene-
sis in something that had happened long ago, that
far-off day day he'd chased a bloodied bank-bandit
all the way to Dreamer's Mountain.

Yet he was still far from fully convinced of this until
Santone snapped his fingers and a door creaked open
in back. Struther Cady sauntered into the barroom
with six-shooters sagging from their holsters and a
cigarette pasted to his brutal underlip.

Now he believed.

Cady drew up a chair and proceeded quietly to
unfold the identical tale he'd related first to Santone
a week earlier. The ex-con seemed totally confident
that, with Tillerman agreeing to guide them to the
exact spot where he'd hunted Lucas McCoy it would
be possible for him to take it from there and figure
out precisely where his ex-partner had stashed the
cache.

'Lucas was dying while you hounded him that day,
Tillerman,' he summarized. 'By then the man was too
sick and weak to try anything fancy with the *dinero*. All
he would have been looking for while you were closing in, was someplace secure. Me and McCoy were
together quite a spell. I knew how he thought. Like I
say, I reckon it would likely be almost easy for me to
figure where he most likely planted the big *dinero* . . .
providing you steer me straight, that is.'

'What choice has the man got?' Santone drawled.
'Simply play along with us to uncover an old haul
with no danger to himself, on one hand, or never get
to see his daughter alive again on the other. What
choice would anybody make? Eh, big man?'

130

Tillerman shook his head like a tormented bear. The immense stress of controlling his rage and his mind-numbing concern for his daughter seemed to be deadening his mind.

At first glance, Cady's confidence in his ability to locate the haul if he were to know the exact course hunted and hunter had followed that day sounded almost ridiculous, impossible.

Yet the intense locked stares of both men as they waited for his reply confirmed that they must have believed it from the outset to have gone to such lengths to force his compliance.

What they had done reeked of criminal thinking and ruthless disregard for innocent people. As well, Santone was plainly also motivated by revenge against Trina. But dogs would bark, it was their nature. Tillerman mustn't fritter time away figuring how this ugly situation had come about, he told himself. Just do what he knew he must.

They'd expected his compliance, and they got it. Naturally he demanded proof that his daughter was still alive but the request was denied.

'You're in no position to demand anything,' Santone said with obvious pleasure as he came up from his chair in one oiled motion. 'Put that fortune in our laps and then we'll talk.'

For a brief while longer Tillerman feigned stubbornness, delaying, playing for time. But they knew they had him. And when Santone began to grow angry, the big man's fear for his daughter forced him to cave in.

He would do what they wanted, he declared. Just

131

as he had known he must since the awful moment when he held that telegram in trembling hands in a hotel room by Sky Cloud Lake.

Cady's smile was the first Tillerman had ever seen on that lined, tough face. Strangely, Santone appeared almost disappointed for the moment as though he might have hoped Tillerman would refuse and so force him to kill him. But the man was soon back to his buoyant self, calling for a round of drinks and snapping his fingers as he had done to summon Cady.

Tillerman stared.

Four men were coming through the door where Cady had first appeared. Gun-toting, cold-eyed and armed to the teeth, their appearance shouted owlhoot – and Tillerman understood at last the reason behind the barkeep's obvious tension upon his arrival.

It was now all too plain that Santone and Cady had overlooked nothing when they sat down to hatch their ugly scheme. They had a hostage, an armed bunch, a treasure to uncover – and now a 'guide dog' with his teeth drawn. He almost had to admire their thoroughness, while any faint hope he'd had of maybe turning the tables either now or later was snuffed out like a candle. The way he saw it now, were he to do everything they demanded, and if by some miracle Cady was to find his dirty money, then and only then might Trina have some slim hope of survival. But if he tried anything reckless? He dare not think of that outcome.

'Should we meet anyone on the trails,' announced

132

Santone, 'we'll say we're helping you find Trina. Is all clear in that mule head of yours, Tillerman?'

'Let's do it,' Tillerman growled, striding for the doors.

'Look at him,' Santone invited the others. 'His lousy life is hanging by a thread, yet he still acts like he's king turtle in the swamp. You know, gents, I was sore when Trina gave me my walking papers. But when I think of taking this bastard on as a father-in-law, why, I guess it just could be she did me the best turn of my life.'

Laughter accompanied the party out into the moonlight. Disarmed, Tillerman led the way from the town. He rode like a man heading for hell.

Caroline greeted the lawman at the door.

'It's so thoughtful of you to stop by, Nate. I . . . I can tell by your face there's no news.'

'None, more's the pity, Caroline,' said Poole, following her into the front room. 'I guess I just came by looking for a few answers.'

'I don't understand.' Tall and regal with her black hair tied in a severe bun on the nape of her neck and disciplined eyes dry of tears, Caroline Tillerman looked every inch the mistress of a great ranch refusing to cave in under intolerable pressure.

Poole stood beneath a heavy chandelier turning his hat in his hands. 'Just wondering if you have any notion what's gotten into Sam,' he said uneasily. 'I guess I don't have to tell you this whole hunt would be operating far better with him calling the shots. You know. Taking charge, blistering eardrums, acting like he was the general and the rest of us just dumb foot-soldiers. You know how he can be. Times like this, that sort of authority really works.'

'I'm sorry, Nate. As you know, I went to town to see him when he didn't show here. I've never seen Sam that way. He was a stranger. But it's typical, isn't it? I've never needed him so desperately, and what does he do? Lets me down, again.'

'I reckon there's more to this than meets the eye, Caroline. Someone reckons they saw him leaving town late. Said he was with some men who seemed to be avoiding the lights.' A pause. 'This citizen had a feeling one of the bunch could have been Santone.'

The blood drained from Caroline's taut cheeks.

'Santone? What are you suggesting, Sheriff?'

'Heck, I'm not even sure—'

'Sam hates Emile Santone. He would never ride with him at a time like this. This gives me an uneasy feeling, Nate. Perhaps you should try and find out where they went, and if it was indeed Sam and Santone.'

'Sorry. I'm on my way to Greasy Grass Flats. We're going to search the old mine-workings there.'

'Aren't they . . . aren't those shafts flooded?'

He avoided her eyes. 'Can't overlook anything, Caroline. Well, if you hear anything of Sam. . . .'

'I won't. How could he do this to me, Nate?'

Nate Poole was a wise man. But even he didn't have an answer to that one.

Sunlight flooded Marble Canyon.

On the day of the robbery Sam Tillerman had feared he'd lost McCoy for good by the time they stormed into this snow-heavy foothill section of Dreamer's Mountain, until he spied movement on a hill flank above. It was just a flicker, but proved to be enough. Surging up through the drifts and rocks, he lost considerable time cross-cutting over the hillside before eventually picking up the clear signs of the outlaw's horse, which led at last to a tell-tale splotch of crimson upon a snowy boulder.

Memories came flooding back now as he led two of the outlaw four, Toomey and Crites, through a thick growth of trees and brush, dotted with pools of clear water supplied by small streams trickling down from a number of springs higher up the canyon. Where sunlight touched the higher walls of Marble Canyon it dramatically altered the hue of the sandstone and limestone walls, stained by water and streaked by iron and salt.

A single trail led to the higher country, a faint track used only by wild animals. And back then, by an outlaw on the run.

On glimpsing the swaying figure of Lucas McCoy a short distance ahead of him on the Blue Hills trail that fateful day, Tillerman had spurred recklessly after the man through the thinning brush. He was pursuing a runaway bank–bandit. There was no thought of money. For together with the possemen far back at Black Rock, he'd sighted Struther Cady climbing the rocks and boulders back there, dragging the bulging bank-sack behind him. Neither then nor later had anyone suspected the outlaws had pulled a switch and that McCoy had made his run for Dreamer's with the entire $20,000.

Today, Tillerman's big head twisted in every direction as he studied the trail leading up for Dead Man's Draw with new eyes. He rode slumped in the saddle like a weary man. But this was only a pose. He was as charged up as a man could be and the gimlet glitter of his eyes afforded sharp contrast to his affected demeanour.

Somewhere between Danziger and the mountain Tillerman had finally jolted out of the sense of almost dazed helplessness that had overtaken him following Trina's abduction.

But at that moment he'd never been more dangerously alert or determined, as he relived events ten years past. He was now evaluating every foot of the unfolding terrain for possible cache sites, and plotting his next moves – which he knew could well be his last.

This was the regular Tillerman, wrenched back from the brink of despair. And now that his unprecedented moment of weakness was behind him his mind hummed with icy clarity and he was in complete control. The way he must be. The way he would be now until they killed him or he killed them.

He was under no illusions.

If he did nothing but play along with Cady and Santone the way they wanted, then both he and Trina must surely die. He was in the company of outlaws and killers who knew full well the penalty for the heinous crime of kidnap. For them, this was a go-for-broke situation: all or nothing. For his daughter's sake, he would have to be cool, calm and lethal. Not some shell-shocked loser allowing the currents of disaster to carry him away.

Great boulders bulked among the trees, and willows leaned over still, clear ponds. He was looking back over the years and envisioning a desperately wounded man heeling his horse downslope for the draw here, hunted and bleeding, with pursuit close in back and a king's ransom in paper money which he must stash before it was too late.

Now that Tillerman understood about the money the reason behind McCoy's desperate run for Red Man's Draw took on a different aspect. It had to be logical now to assume that the only reason the dying badman had braved this rough terrain had been to find his hiding-place.

He glanced back.

Hawk-faced Crites and blocky Toomey were temporarily out of sight. Which meant that, with the other owlhoots, Murch and Catt, scouting ahead, and Santone and Cady on the far side of the bluff, searching the small caverns there, Tillerman was alone in the flooding heat and drooping growth.

There was no necessity for the outlaws to keep him under close watch. He dare not try anything and they knew it. He was not about to try and cut and run. He could have done that a dozen times had he been prepared to give up on the hostage.

The reality was that he was shackled here as securely as if Santone were leading him around by a chain in his nose like a performing bear.

The draw didn't look anything special at first. The mouth opened up off to his right, short, steep-walled and thickly littered with slabs of talus fallen from higher up.

But as he reined in to look around, Tillerman felt a tingle of the nerve-ends as he once again tried to place himself in Lucas McCoy's boots that day. Leaking blood like a sieve; packing a big piece of cash; some outsized rancher with a gun pressing him close. And back at Black Rock, Cady relying on him to survive, hole up someplace, get strong, come back and spring him, then return here for the money.

Caves or gopher holes or suchlike would be too obvious if anyone was to come searching out here, he figured. He must search for something natural-looking, casual. And what looked more that way than a litter of talus slabs scattered about exactly as they'd crashed down from the iron-stained cliff face above?

They would surely have protruded above the snow. . . .

'Hey, Tillerman. Where are you?'

Toomey's shout echoed hollowly.

'Check out that rock pool over by the dead cotton-wood!' Tillerman called back. 'I've got some brush here needs a second look.'

But they weren't buying. He swore softly as he detected the sounds of their horses closing in from the east, the way they had all ridden up.

Tillerman gave himself the shaved tip of a second to make a decision, then booted the horse into a star-tled run.

He rode directly by the branch canyon, raking the horse with spur and lifting it into a lope. Toomey and Crites started in yelling for him to hold up as they came crashing through the brush. Tillerman kept on for several minutes before cutting sharply into a stand of cottonwoods where concealing limbs trailed the ground and hid him from sight, where the stony earth left no sign.

The hellions went rushing by. He gave them a minute then backtrailed to reach the draw again. Swinging down, he rushed forward and began over-turning pieces of talus in feverish haste, working hard at convincing himself that, cache-wise, McCoy could not have found a more suitable spot for his purposes. One by one he hurled the pieces aside, all the while keeping both ears cocked for the sound of returning hoofbeats.

He stopped abruptly on sighting what appeared to be the corner of a slicker peeking out from beneath a motley-colored chunk of fallen rock the size of a table top. With some effort he heaved it aside, and there it was. Tightly wrapped in the protecting oilskin were four saddle-bags stuffed tight with banknotes with rocks underneath to keep them up out of the seepage.

It was a breathtaking moment in which down-to-earth, no-nonsense Sam Tillerman was convinced that God, destiny, Lady Luck or sheer fool's fortune had smiled upon him at last. He felt the exhilaration rush through his veins as he hefted his prize and legged it back to the horse. Everything was up for grabs now with the outcome of the whole game rest-ing on how the dice rolled in the next minutes. And how he chose to roll them.

He'd barely hit leather when the head and shoul-ders of ugly Willis Crites appeared above a clump of brush some fifty yards south.

'What the freak are you doin', Tillerman? And what you got there, anyways?'

Apart from twenty grand, what Tillerman had was desperation and no weapons. But he did have a good horse. An exceptional horse.

He took off north without response and wild yells signalled the beginning of the chase.

He covered maybe a quarter-mile at headlong speed before cutting into a stand of trees, where he sprang down and hit the ground running. There was barely time enough to string a riata across the choked trail between two trees before Crites and Toomey came roaring up along the canyon floor, cursing and red-faced in the heat.

They hit the taut rope hard, Toomey back-flipping from his saddle and Crites catching it across the belly and somersaulting over it.

One blow from a melon-sized rock to the back of his head as he tried to rise from the ground stretched Willis Crites senseless. Tillerman snatched up the outlaw's Colt and rammed it against Hunk Toomey's thick neck while the man was still on hands and knees with blood running from a gash in the side of his head. Toomey stared up in dazed incomprehension. In fringed buckskin jacket and boiled pink shirt, Tillerman appeared grizzly-bear huge and sidewinder-mean as the Colt in his hand clicked on to full cock.

'You're taking me to the girl, trash. Ain't that right?'

'No goddamn way!'

Tillerman smashed the man so hard with the barrel that for a bad moment he feared he'd killed him. There was one quick way to find out. He drove a boot into the man's ribs. Toomey groaned and his eyelids fluttered. Tillerman prised his teeth open with the gun muzzle.

'Right?'

Toomey's bloodied head nodded. Right.

CHAPTER 9

BITTER BLOOD

Emile Santone's buckskin was fighting to veer away from the giant deadfall but the rider would not allow it. At the very last moment the racing animal realized it had no choice. It took off and the rider lifted it expertly so that the hind hoofs no more than snicked timber, and they were across and running again. There was no way that Cady, Murch or Catt were about to attempt that white-knuckle leap; not even for $20,000. Instead the trio were forced to cut their lathered cayuses back to a trot and pick their way through scattered boulders either side of the dead-fall, by which time Santone was almost out of sight across the afternoon hills, still riding like a demon in pursuit of that sifting column of butter-coloured dust drifting away from the pass.

Tillerman's dust.

Nursing a cracked head and unable to ride, Willis Crites had been left back at Marble Canyon to recover or die, whatever he pleased. But the hardcase had recovered sufficiently to inform the others he'd seen Tillerman with weathered saddle-bags strapped to his saddle taking off across the bluff above Redman's Draw with his gun at Toomey's back.

It was next door to impossible to believe that Tillerman had located the cache, got the jump on Crites and Toomey, then side-slipped Santone and Cady to bust clear of the canyon and and set up a long head start, all in the space of several minutes.

But what else could they believe?

Tillerman and Toomey were cutting straight across country to the north-east. North-east lay Pinto Canyon, the sun was sliding towards the western rim and the horses flew so swiftly they barely appeared to touch the baked hide of Turlock County.

The outlaw named Lat Court stirred so sharply that his silver spurs jangled. Trina calculated her jailer to be somewhere in his middle twenties, alleycat-lean and wearing yellow roper's gloves and a blanket coat with buckskin patches on the elbows.

He was as efficient-looking as a bayonet and the girl had quickly realized why Santone had chosen him to stay back with her when he and the others had disappeared.

'Thought I heard somethin',' the man drawled, moving to the entrance to stare down into the darkening canyon. He turned his head to stare at the girl through eyes the same colour as his gloves. 'You hear anythin'?'

'Only your knees knocking.'

The sawed-off had not left the outlaw's gloved

hands since he had been left in charge in this big old chamber of stone and crumbling adobe halfway up the ancient cliff face. For a moment the twin barrels were raised to cover Trina Tillerman, then angled at the floor again.

'You got too much of your big-ass old man in you, sister. Anyone ever told you that?'

'It's not like you to pay compliments, convict.'

'Ain't no compliment,' he sneered. 'Big Sam? Big Nothin' would fit better. Your daddy's the breed of high-steppin' whoremaster I've been tanglin' with all my life. They got everythin' and want more. They got dough, power, friends in high places. The law's in their pocket and they all think they got an honest-to-go right to lord it over—'

The badman's gun wavered momentarily in his hands as sounds rose from the canyon floor. Down below, a horse had whickered sharply. But Lat Court knew his horses, and that sound had not come from his mare nor his hostage's brown colt.

In an instant he had doused the lantern and taken up his position in an archway in which the chieftains of the Ancient Ones had once stood in ceremonial robes to hurl shrieking maidens to the rocks below to appease the Pima gods. Nothing stirred in the velvet night.

Then: 'Lat! It's me. Toomey!'

Court's neck hair lifted as he raised his sawed-off to his shoulder.

'Show yourself, Toomey. Where in hell did you come from anyway? Where's Santone?' Trina noted the man asked after Santone. Not Cady. She had noted everything about her captors since the outset, slotting away every detail for future reference. It had quickly become obvious following her capture out along the Monroe Road, that even if Struther Cady regarded himself and Santone as equal partners in their vile enterprise, the man she had once thought she loved was really the *numero uno*.

Emile had always been commanding and impressive. But freed of sober restraints and role-playing, he'd emerged like a malevolent moth from its chrysalis as a different and vastly more sinister species.

'I got a message,' called Toomey. 'I'm comin' up.'

His eyes accustoming to the gloom, a tense Court eventually picked out Toomey's bulky shape creaking its way up the peeled-pole ladder which provided the only way up or down. In the old times, the Pimas would draw up their ladders when their enemies came calling. Court thus far had no awareness that, concealed behind Toomey's bulk, an enemy as formidable as any that had once menaced the Ancient Ones was drawing closer with every protesting groan of sun-dried poles lashed together with rawhide strips.

Hunk Toomey was relying totally upon trigger-happy Court spotting Tillerman beneath him. He was leaking vast amounts of icy sweat as he anticipated the moment when he must throw himself to one side and rely upon his henchman's marksmanship to blast Tillerman into hell while missing him. How wide a pattern did those old Remingtons throw, anyway?

The climbers were within thirty feet of the packed-clay landing. Now twenty. Toomey suddenly cracked.

'Tillerman!' he screamed and swayed his body away to one side to afford Court a clear line of fire.

Court and Tillerman triggered simultaneously, and neither missed. Tillerman gasped as a searing pain ripped his side. He was forced to hang on fiercely as Toomey kicked down at him, trying to dislodge him. Something plummeted past the struggling pair and Lat Court's lazily turning shotgun followed him down as the outlaw smashed into the floor far below, the sawed-off clattering away and firing again in a brilliant burst of crimson and hot orange that lighted up a hundred yards of canyon.

A boot crunched Tillerman's neck and shoulder. Somehow he hung on, shoving the Colt upwards to make contact with muscle-packed flesh before triggering twice. Lucky for Tillerman he hooked both powerful arms around the rungs as Toomey's sagging body crashed down fully upon him, spilling blood over his shoulder.

'You mongrel bastard, Tillerman. . . .'

Tillerman bucked upwards with all his might and the outlaw was sent flying, arms and legs pumping and his scream choking in his throat as he vanished in the darkness beneath.

The thud of contact trembled the ladder.

Tillerman began clawing his slow way upwards when a hand reached out and clutched his collar.

'Father! Father, I knew you'd come!'

Trina was alive!

Somehow this realization invested Tillerman with the strength he had to summon in order to struggle on to the high landing, where he passed out.

'Get up there!' hissed Santone, his yellow thatch all that was clearly visible of him in the thick gloom of the canyon floor. 'Tillerman hasn't raised the ladder, which proves he's hit, just like I said. Well, what are you waiting for, damnit?'

Abraham Catt was crouched in a patch of filtering starlight. He had a gun in either hand, a black dash of moustache, an earring in each ear and a poker-chip clasp holding his bandanna together at the throat. He had all these things along with a violent case of the shakes.

'Jesus, Emile,' he panted, 'you just seen what happened to Lat and Toomey. A man would be a sitting duck tryin' to get up that ladder now—'

'You mean a sitting duck – like you are here right now?'

Santone's six-gun muzzle rested against the fancy green poker-chip clasp at the badman's brown throat to add emphasis to the chill of his words. But a hand reached from the gloom to push the weapon down.

'Easy, Santone,' counselled Cady. 'We're losing men at a rate of knots. We've got the numbers, he's got no place to go, it's all our way. We don't have to commit suicide to nail Tillerman to the cross. Anyway, we know the bastard's hit, so let's take a little time, huh?'

The gun in Santone's hand flicked to cover his partner. In the space of several hours the outlaw

147

from Utah had shed his last snake's skin of cover to emerge as what he had always been. Pure killer. At that moment Cady, Murch and Catt were in far greater danger from this yellow-haired gunpacker than from Sam Tillerman or the hunting posses, and they knew it. Tillerman's daring breakout from Red Man's Draw and the loss of half their force had aroused more than Santone's fury. His vanity and pride were affronted in a way lesser men couldn't understand. The killer was raging, and only blood and money could assuage him.

'Duck!' someone shouted hysterically and all four hurled themselves for cover as something came hurtling down from the Pimas' lair to hit the earth with a solid smack of sound. A canyon wind fluttered banknotes across Cady's outstretched legs.

He sat up and grabbed at the money incredulously as a big voice drifted down.

'You win in the end, scum!' Tillerman's voice boomed. 'Take it and get. And may it bring you all the evil luck you deserve.'

The badmen were on their feet, hooting and dancing and snatching up wads of banknotes from the burst bag. Cady was first to notice that Santone did not join in. He shoved a thousand-dollar wad inside his shirt and clapped his partner on the shoulder with a huge grin.

'Emile, don't you *compre?* We've won, man. We're on our way. We'll be out of Colorado come sun-up—'

'You've got to be kidding!'

The way Santone spat out that line saw Catt and Murch quit pounding one another's shoulders. They turned to stare at the Nevadan open-mouthed, not even beginning to understand. They had the money. What else was there?

'She made me look a fool,' Santone said in an unsteady voice, all shoulders and golden head in the half-light. 'Dumped me like I was some pimply-faced schoolkid hanging on to her petticoat. Her bitching mother told the whole world she'd rather die than see me get one dime, then hauled in the attorneys to make it fair, square and legal.'

He paused to massage his jaw which still ached from a knockout punch delivered upon a crowded street. Blue eyes were ice as he stared upwards.

'They've got to pay . . . the big man, the bitch daughter . . . the snob mother. That's how it's got to be before we can claim a win. . . .' His gaze dropped. 'Relax, Catt. I've decided you're not up to it. This calls for someone with real balls. Struther, *amigo*, the big man's yours.'

To the bewilderment of Catt and Murch, Cady stood motionless for a long moment, then moved to the ladder. The pair thought the ex-con had suddenly turned yellow. Not so. Ten years inside had given Cady a deep insight into the make-up of true danger men, such as Santone. He knew instinctively that his prospects would be far better climbing that ladder to confront Big Sam Tillerman than tangling with his partner in crime in his present frame of mind. They were but coyotes and scavengers of the glittering deserts and snowplain wilderness, but Santone was a wolf.

Slowly he began to ascend.

149

CHAPTER 10

THE SURVIVORS

'I can do it, and so can you, Father. All we have to do is slide down the chute and it will bring us out up-canyon from them. We can just steal away afoot and simply disappear.'

'I'm too big for any goddamn chute built for itsy-bitsy Pimas,' panted Tillerman. 'Besides, Sam Tillerman's not running from any low-life bunch of tenth-raters any longer. I offered them a fair deal, they turned it down, now they are just going to have to pay. That's how it's got to be, honey.'

'Don't honey me, you . . . you anachronism!'

Tillerman sat up straighter against the stone wall, his scowl coming down hard over uncomprehending eyes. Their tender reunion hadn't lasted very long, he noted cynically. Ten minutes and she was back to acting like a man again. And he knew who he had to thank for that.

'If you are going to insult your father, do it in English.'

'All right, you are a throwback. A dinosaur. You belong in the Dark Ages. You command and all must obey. Women are insignificant in your eyes – even when you lavish on them. It was wonderful what you did tonight, coming after me. Now you're spoiling it all by continuing to play Big Sam right to the final curtain, never mind what happens to either of us.'

'By glory, your mother's warped you so fierce that I doubt anything will ever straighten you o—'

'Mother is a saint and you're just a—'

'A dinosaur. Yeah, I heard. Well, this dinosaur's still got his teeth, Miss Smartmouth.'

Trina straightened and stepped back from him, smoothing her skirt.

'I'm going down that escape chute, Father, either with or without you.'

'Go ahead, leave me. You mother did, why not y—'

His words dried up. He was talking to himself. In one smooth flash of long limbs and frilly underdrawers, his daughter had vanished into the dark, man-made slipway leading down.

For a moment his shoulders slumped and his six-gun clunked against the floor. He knew all about the escape chutes in these ancient cliff dwellings, had inspected them often in his early ranching days when he'd come this far afield searching for strays to stock his acres. But he'd been telling the truth when claiming they were far too small for someone of his bulk. Trina might just make it . . . and his face sagged with anguish as he pictured her slipping out into that outlaw-peopled canyon below, alone, unarmed and fearful. His little girl. . . .

The ladder creaked.

Tillerman sucked a huge draft of air into his lungs and rose in a crouch. He was hurt but could still fight. He could still make it hot and heavy enough, not to survive maybe, but with luck he might last long enough to give Trina time to get away. That would satisfy him. Maybe that cantankerous ex-wife of his would give him some posthumous credit if he were able to achieve that, although he doubted it.

'Tillerman?'

He recognized Cady's voice, hoarse and roughened by countless jailhouse nights.

'You've got me, Cady,' he croaked theatrically, raising the gleaming gun barrel. His grip was rock steady. 'If you just let my little girl go, I'll hand in my gun. . . .'

He darted to the wall. Cady was some ten feet below the landing. They triggered together. Pain bit Tillerman's thigh like the jaws of a snapping turtle. He triggered again and the outlaw plummeted to the moneybags far below with a faint slap of sound.

An angry volley raked his eyrie and Tillerman was down. He'd known pain before but this was the kind to turn your hair white.

He must have passed out.

Again!

When he came to he found himself alone inside the long chamber with light filtering through crumbling walls and shaped casements. Evidently he'd crawled inside to escape the whine and snarl of the ricochets coming off the stone half-dome overhead before losing consciousness. Had he dreamed it, or had he and Caroline just been walking the back range on an early spring morning? It began to seem more like a nightmare than a dream when he stared about at the tendrils of gunsmoke drifting up from below and felt the ravenous she-bear chewing at his side while her cubs feasted on his thigh.

He beat away the critters created by his feverish imagination and felt his whole body tingle with the sudden awareness of actual danger.

The sensation was so overpowering that it succeeded in dragging him back from the unconsciousness that was trying to suck him down into its black guts. Walls rippled and bulged in his vision but he concentrated with a fierce and defiant will. Dug into himself for every reserve and felt his vision slowly clear and feeling return to hands and fingers to realize the shooting had ceased.

Why?

Then the gun bellowed close and the ricochet sang viciously from the wall over his head.

Another.

By the gunblast's flare he made out the distinctive lithe shape rushing across the landing from the ladder. It was Santone in full attack mode, unscathed, closing in for the kill, eager to claim the trophy for himself. Big Sam, stuffed and mounted upon his wall. What a conversation piece for cold winter nights. . . .

Tillerman felt his mind sliding out from under again. The floor all about him glistened with his blood. He triggered and rolled sideways, the pain almost lifting his scalp. Although he anticipated return fire it still came so swiftly that it surprised him. The bullet whammed into a pillar and keened eerily from it while the deep throated thunder of the report filled the chamber and hammered Tillerman's ears.

Quiet again.

His eyes roamed his smoke-hazed surrounds. But there was now no sign of the enemy, and there would be no sound from that cat-footed killer when he came at him again. Light-headed visions of places and people fought to take over his mind but he was still Big Sam, still as determined to fight the awful weakness within himself as the enemy without.

'This is better than all the *dinero*, Tillerman. Money goes, but burying you and both of them will keep me warm every night of my life. . . .'

Tillerman blasted at the sound of the voice, immediately regretted it. He sensed the return fire coming before Santone jerked trigger. He threw himself flat and hugged the crimsoned floor as bullets lanced and screamed overhead. The deafening volley ceased and he was on his feet, one hand grabbing his side, dragging one leg like a cripple. Yet the gun still sprouted from the hand extended before him and every instinct insisted he'd seen that lithe figure vanish through the blinding smoke, that it hadn't been imagination.

A pale face stole a peek around a rock stanchion. Tillerman's bullet screamed off the rock and fragments lacerated Santone's face. The outlaw tilted, off balance, went down shooting as Tillerman used up his last bullet. Santone's fine Colt dropped into the rubble as he tried to rise. For long seconds he stared up at the figure of Tillerman which was assuming vast proportions in his distorting vision. He raised a hand as though in farewell, then clenched it into a fist and whispered, 'Big man!' He rolled dead on to his back.

It was over, but why was the canyon night full of gun thunder? That was Tillerman's last puzzling thought as he fell like one of his big redwoods.

The San Rafael medico quit the sickroom in a huff.

'He's all yours, ladies,' he said, snapping shut his fat and shiny black bag. 'And you're welcome. I'll waive my fee in this case on the proviso that you never seek to enlist my services for your husband and father again.'

Caroline and Trina stood looking thoughtful as the good physician vanished with a swirl of coat-tails and a jiggling of the pince nez. They traded glances, almost amused that the high drama of Pima Canyon should seem to have faded so swiftly to be replaced by the practical everyday concerns of its aftermath.

Nate Poole had been out earlier to visit his old friend and secure from Tillerman and Trina the details of both the battle and their daring escape from the canyon. The lawman was wide-eyed with wonder as he realized how close it had been when Trina had made contact with the passing search party, which had then succeeded in dealing with what was left of the outlaws in the canyon after Big Sam had dealt with Santone a hundred feet above.

Sam had fought with the sheriff also.

They'd never had him as a patient before; he was worse than they could have imagined.

They knew it. So did Big Sam. But of all the ambitions he'd cherished in his life, being a good patient was not even listed. And now he chose to excel himself as he listened to the doctor's buggy wheel away from the house and clatter through the gate, while he rose and stuffed his shirt into his pants. He was loaded down with strapping and limping like an old, old man, yet was now bellowing like a yearling bull under the cutting knife.

'Whiskey! What's a man got to do to get a whiskey in his own house, goddamnit?'

'It's not your house any longer, Father,' Trina reminded. 'And I do wish you would not shout at Mother that way.'

'Don't start me up,' Tillerman warned, lowering himself to lean against a low bureau which creaked beneath his great weight. 'You disobeyed me out there at the canyon, miss. I said you weren't to go and—'

'I saved your wretched life!' Trina cut in, stamping her foot. She whirled on Caroline. 'Honestly, mother, nothing has changed, has it.'

'I rather think you're right,' Caroline replied. But her tone was gentle; there was no fire in her Irish blue eyes. 'Er, where are you going, dear?'

'To my room,' Trina snapped from the doorway. 'I need some peace and quiet to decide whether I'll have to leave.'

'Don't bother!' Tillerman shot back, clutching at his pants. 'Getting shot to hell is a picnic to putting up with your high and mighty ways. You stay, miss, I'm leaving.'

'Neither of you is leaving,' Caroline cut in, voice and manner reflecting all her full mistress-of-Tadpole-authority now as she went to Tillerman's side.

'We're finished leaving this ranch. All of us. Trina, go make coffee and biscuits for three. No arguments. And you – Mr Tillerman – you come with me if you think you can walk thirty yards without passing out.'

Somehow he made it with her to the South Room. But he didn't like it. He stood at her side gazing up at the life-sized picture above the hearth.

'So?' he growled.

'Lovely, isn't it?'

'Look, Mrs Tillerman, if you think you can parley a little excitement and a few bullet holes into something fancy, then you can—'

She turned to him, holding his hands. He had not see that look in her eyes in years.

'You don't have to pretend, Samuel. When you were unconscious, you whispered my name over and over again for hours. You said you loved me, and I think I've always known I would need to get you half dead and out of your head to admit it. What's wrong? Aren't you going to explode?'

'I said all that? You know, I think I remember . . .' His features softened as he leaned against the fireplace mantel. In and out of consciousness as he'd been for days, he found he was remembering things like her tenderness, his desperate need of her. Other things as well. . . .

'Tell me, woman, did I have visitors one day. . . ?'

'You did. The State Railway president came to pay his respects and ask you to represent them in an insurance matter, and there was Mr Mallone, the Association president, who couldn't wait for you to recover to offer you a contract. . . .'

'Sure,' he half-grinned. 'Now I recall. And I told them to go to hell, didn't I?'

Caroline smiled.

'Yes, you did. They were both very upset, but I was proud. You . . . you told them that you were all through chasing your own tail – as you put it – handling big deals. Said you just wanted to be a cowman and work in dirty boots all day. Do you recall that?'

He realized he did recall.

'Every word . . .' he said wonderingly. 'And I meant it. It was like I was just sick enough to tell myself to shut up and figure out about what I really want . . .' His eyes were on her face. 'Do you reckon I had to get shot up and sick before I could see that . . . that all I really wanted was to come back here and pick up where . . . or maybe that's way too late, Cal?'

'It's never too late, Samuel.' She hadn't called him that in years. 'And I'll never forget what you said about us when you thought you were dying.'

'Nor . . . nor will I. . . .'

He seemed to stoop a little. Suddenly it didn't seem important to be big and commanding. Nor lonesome. As lonesome as Sam Tillerman knew he had been in his heart all those years. His voice was tender.

'Cal, oh Cal.'

She came into his arms and it ended there beneath the forgiving eyes of their young selves gazing down understandingly from the high South Room wall.